FALSE START

Notes From The Deep End

DANIELLA BLUE

OLIVERHEBERBOOKS

To Lisa...best sister ever!!

ONE

Re: Availability Feb 4

December 27, 2:47 am

Dear Mrs. Harriman,

*Just sending this email to let you know that I did receive
your letters. All six of them in fact, including the two certified and the one sent through the University. I also got your
voicemails, Facebook messages and the DMs on my Instagram. I'm sorry but I'm just not interested in participating
in whatever you have planned. And it's not what you think.
It's not a fear thing or that I don't support the cause, it's
simply the timing of it all doesn't allow me to leave Los
Angeles.*

*As you know, I'm a full-time college student now. My
classwork combined with my responsibilities in the beach
house I share with my friends requires focused commitment.
In addition, I'm a Division One Swimmer (NCAA Cham-
pion two years running) and I volunteer as a mentor at the
Dunes (my rehabilitation facility if you remember) when I*

can. Not that I plan on becoming a therapist or anything, but who knows? My major is still undeclared as of this correspondence.

If I had any spare time over the past few years, it's been spent raising money for a foundation in my friend, Annie Madsen's, name. Maybe you remember her? She's the Olympic swimmer who died of leukemia a few years back. Anyway, "Art for Annie" is this grassroots project where a bunch of local artists here in Los Angeles donate works and sell them for cancer research. It's no March of Dimes or UNICEF but we've made a few bucks for the cause. We're currently planning a Valentine's Day black tie auction to fundraise for it. Fancy food, ice sculptures, a classy band, the whole works. I even arranged for a highly-regarded party planner to organize it. I have out of town friends flying in and press lined up. So you see, I'm spread very thin and there is just no way I could spare the time to make the trip.

Please wish the others well. Tell them I support them and I'm sorry there isn't more than one of me. I hope they understand...

I'M NOT a huge fan of sweaty bare feet on sand. Like if you take your sneakers off and you step onto the beach for a stroll, it's gross. The sand sticks to your soles, and it gets stuck between your toes. But it's not like wearing shoes is any less annoying. Your balance is off, it takes extra effort, you can't go in the water. A beach walk is something to be enjoyed. The warmth, the beautiful scenery around you. But if you can't trust your footing...one false step...

I stood at the edge of the patio, sandals dangling from my fingers, watching the dance floor at Starlight Beach Club like it was some kind of movie I hadn't been cast in. The DJ—some guy who called himself SoundSexy, which, okay—was deep into a playlist he'd labeled "Holiday Chill...But Also Danceable," and to be fair, he kind of nailed it. Slow jammed enough for swaying hips and drink-in-hand energy but also dance tracks that had the place vibrating. People were everywhere. My swim teammates here to support the cause, Dunes people, friends. There were randos lounging in beach chairs, clustered near the fire pits or in the darkness on the VIP deck. It smelled like coconut oil and sweat all dramatically enhanced by the golden flicker of the tiki torches and the string lights hanging above...

And me? I was here for it. But not totally there.

"Why aren't you out dancing?" Staci asked, sliding up beside me with her third fruity rainbow something-or-other mocktail of the night. "This is your party. Enjoy yourself."

I shrugged. "Just taking it in."

"Well, you look amazing. I knew you'd rock that dress. Blue is so your color."

I gave a good tug at the tight knot of my halter top. Sophisticated and playful, Staci had promised. Short and tight, reality corrected. My hair was clipped up, safe from my neck, and my makeup held firm thanks to Ari's industrial strength setting spray. I actually liked my three-inch silver wedges. Stable, stylish, and gave me some height on my five-foot frame. That is, until my feet turned numb and I had to take them off.

Staci on the other hand was all confidence in her golden cocktail dress with her red hair long and glossy like a freaking mermaid. Three years ago, she was shooting up in gas station bathrooms. Tonight? Co-hosting a fundraising beach party under the stars. I hated to mellow her excitement.

"There are a ton of people here," I said brightly. "Press people and cameras. More than I thought."

"Are you kidding?" Staci laughed. "You're still a celebrity

who draws attention. Although, after today's big Damian Cross murder press conference, I wondered if they'd be worn out. But hey, free drinks, private club, and moonlight over the Pacific? Not a hard sell."

"You've gone full PR girl, haven't you?"

"Lance is pretty happy too." She nodded to her boyfriend of three years who was chatting it up with a reporter. He wore some stylish combo of cargo pants and a vintage Metallica rock tee with red nail polish, gears in his ears, and his hair in a super neat manbun. "Some news story just placed him on a top ten list of Who's Who in Young American Artists. I'm super proud of him."

"He couldn't have done it without you, you know."

Before she could respond, Janessa and Ari weaved through the crowd. Ari's white tank dress hugged her tanned skin perfectly while Janessa opted for a pink tube top number that showed off her swimmer shoulders. Her long dark braids were held back by a blinking pink scrunchie.

"Girl, you'd think I'd be in good shape from swimming." Janessa laughed. "But man do my feet hurt."

"And I'm so happy I wasn't scheduled to fly this weekend!" Ari said, still giggling from whatever Janessa had just whispered. "I haven't been to a thing like this since I stopped blacking out at them."

"You know this isn't a dry party," I warned, nodding toward the tiki bar. "Read your labels. Virgins are clearly marked."

"Right side's safe," Staci added with a wink. "Speaking of drinks, Nat. You look like you could use one. Maybe an energy one. The night is still young."

"Hey." Ari bumped my shoulder. "Shouldn't you be hanging with your golden boy?"

"What?" I blinked. "Where?"

"Eero," she teased. "You know, tall, European, very into you?"

"He and Lance are chatting with the press now," Staci chimed in, her berry-colored lips teasing her straw. "They want to get that out of the way so they can focus on the afterhours beach volleyball game tonight. They're recruiting dream teams last I heard, so everyone better prepare themselves."

I was suddenly jolted back to reality by a hand gripping my arm.

"Oh my God, Natalie, is this French onion dip?" Cassidy stared at me, her blue eyes wide with urgency. She pointed toward the food table set up near the tiki torches, a spread of snacks and appetizers artfully arranged on driftwood platters. "It looks like it might be, with the little chunks in it, and Kevin doesn't want to make a scene!"

Kevin, our beloved Onion Boy, stood a short distance away in his floral button-down shirt and khaki shorts, glaring at the veggie tray like it had personally wronged him. His shaggy dark blond bangs hung low over his eyes. The rest of us exchanged a look, silently challenging one another not to dissolve into laughter.

"His new greatest fear is to end up in veggie dip," Cassidy explained, as though it made perfect sense even to those of us whose brains hadn't been scrambled by years of synthetic drugs. Strangely, we all knew exactly what she meant. Even after three years clean, Kevin still believed he was an onion and lived in constant terror of being peeled. A crisis? Maybe. But honestly, a little Onion Boy meltdown would be a great distraction for me.

"Do you think they have any ranch dressing?" Cassidy asked. "Kevin says eating ranch dressing offers a forcefield of protection from harm."

"A forcefield of protection?" Ari echoed, raising an eyebrow.

Cassidy leaned in closer, lowering her voice as though sharing classified information. "We've been watching a lot of conspiracy theory documentaries lately. I know it sounds crazy," she said with a helpless shake of her head. "Sometimes I think he loses touch with reality."

Her assessment of Kevin was ironic, considering she was the one who thought life was a television show. Even her cute, flowered sundress had a discreet pocket sewn in just to hold the remote she carried to "control life" with a click of a button.

"So, what should we do?" Staci asked. "Do you want me to go grab a special plate or something? Kevin trusts me."

"That's okay. I'm just going to bring him a bowl of ranch dressing and let him eat it with a spoon." Cassidy blew a tendril out of her eyes with exasperation. "Men."

We watched as Cassidy headed back to Kevin, who was carefully stacking a plate with broccoli, carrots, and other non-threatening veggies. There was something oddly bittersweet about the fact that I wouldn't have to keep up with Kevin's bizarre dietary rules anymore, now that he was moving back home to Arizona.

"I'll secure the ranch." I offered. "I could use a time out."

"We'll all go. I have to check on desserts anyway," Staci said. "And don't worry. Kevin's only here for the party. Cassidy is with us for the weekend though. I thought it would be nice to get her out of the group home for a while, especially with Kevin leaving for good."

The kitchen at Starlight was brighter and quieter despite the clanking dishes and the hum of the dishwashers. A perfect decibel. Loud noises, especially ones where I didn't readily know the source, annoyed me lately. But the alternative of silence made my brain too loud, so the goal was hovering between the two. I appreciated a good balance when I found it. With the encouragement of that slight glow up, I found a big fridge in the back and spooned some ranch dressing into a ceramic bowl I pulled from a drying rack. Mission accomplished. The girls and I headed back out to the patio.

The four of us stopped short when we ran into a wall of people converging in the corner by the VIP deck. "What's going on over there?" Staci asked.

Ari shrugged. "I don't know. Maybe someone important is here."

Staci stood on her tiptoes, trying to get a better look over the crowd. "I wouldn't be surprised. Lance has done a bunch of projects for some really high-profile people lately."

I licked a drop of ranch from my finger as I half-ass tried to scope out the mob. That's when I saw them...

Holly and Mitch.

Oh. Hell. No.

Mitch leaned against the railing in a white button-down, the sleeves casually rolled to his forearms and the top two buttons undone. The ocean breeze caught the fabric just enough to ripple it across his military-enhanced chest. His blond hair was a little shaggy, like he'd skipped his last trim, but his clean-shaven face allowed a full view of his warm dimpled smile.

Holly clung to his side with her arm lazily slung around his waist. She wore a yellow sundress that seemed to glimmer in silver light and her long chestnut hair spilled in glossy waves down her bare back. She was saying something to the reporter standing in front of them, but her gaze never drifted far from Mitch's face, smiling with that soft, practiced sweetness of hers. So fucking adoring. Attentive. The reporter nodded, scribbled something, then walked off toward the valet.

"Wow, Holly Inez is out?" Ari asked, her tone dripping with disbelief. "I thought they said today on the news she was in custody."

"No, that's her friend," Staci corrected. "You know, the one who drove her Bentley into Ralph Lauren a few months back."

Holly's fingers lingered on his arm, her touch light yet possessive. Holly was taller than me by at least four inches but still Mitch towered over her with his imposing six-three frame. The size difference between us always made me feel safe and oddly confident. I wondered if it did her. She sure looked that way and I hated the pang of jealousy that flared deep within me. I couldn't let it show. Not here. Not now.

"Does Holly actually have a job other than to be rich and party?" Janessa asked.

"She spends a lot of time at Damian Cross' mansion," Ari replied. "Her brother, Brody Inez, is that military survivalist guy with that TV show. He's Damian Cross' partner or whatever."

Staci shook her head. "Man, she's the last person I would expect Mitch to be talking to."

"Why did they even show up?" I asked everyone and no one.

"Lance probably," Staci said, and I could tell by her voice she was being careful with her words. "Mitch comes to the gallery now and then and they hang out. And I'm sure Mitch still supports the cause."

The girls headed back into the crowd, but I lingered. Maybe I was being dramatic. Probably I was. The way he slid his large hand around her small waist. How she stood on her toes just to get to his ear. She whispered something. God knows what. A secret, a tease. Something deep and sensual. He smiled as her fingertips grazed his chest, so light and so fucking intimately.

The kind of touch I'd never mastered.

Why couldn't I do that like her? Relate to a man that boldly? I wanted to reach for someone without flinching, feel warm in their heat, lean into their whisper without hearing an echo of someone else's voice in my head.

Mitch's eyes fluttered as she kissed his neck. Her long pink acrylic nails dragged through his shaggy blond hair. My own fingers tightened around the bowl I was holding. My stomach dropped. My throat closed...

When his gaze found mine, something flickered in his expression. Couldn't name it, but it embarrassed me. Like I'd been caught observing a dark and devious crime...

"Hey, there you are!" Eero's arm slipped around my waist, and he playfully kissed the top of my head. "Where you been? They set up a volleyball net on the beach. Lance and I are making teams. You in?"

I laughed, flat and forced. "I thought that was a late-night, back-at-the-beach-house activity?"

"We can play there too. You know my performance peaks after hours anyway." His crooked smile told me he was up to his usual "goodtime" shenanigans. He'd already given up his trendy nightclub fit for the white shorts and grey tank top ensemble he sported now. His gaze drifted over my shoulder. "Hey, isn't that the girl who is part of that whole Damian Cross case? Like she helped murder him or something?"

"Huh?" I turned to look and pretended I had no idea what he was talking about.

"She was there at his mansion the night of his murder, right?" he asked. "And who's the guy with her?"

A crowd had circled back around them. "I don't know. No idea."

"It looks like she's gonna make a meal out of him later."

Eero laughed at his own joke, already moving on and completely unaware he'd just confirmed the thing I didn't want to believe. I stayed where I was, clutching my bowl of ranch like a shield.

"Natalie, come on," Eero called. "Lance is waiting and we gotta put on a good show."

I looked down at myself, assessing how I would be doing anything athletic dressed as I was. I also realized I was standing in the sand, bare feet half-buried, cold and now damp from the ocean air.

And all I could think was—

This is what it feels like when you can't trust your footing.

Or anything else for that matter.

TWO

Dear Marradine
December 28th 5:27am

So last night went...well it went. It felt strange to be the center of attention again. When I think back to my Olympic freak out four years ago, it's like watching a movie in my head. Actors playing out a scene that isn't real... You probably know what I mean, right? I've always wondered, is it strange for someone like you to watch yourself on film? Being someone who isn't you?

Sometimes I feel like an imposter. In my head I have a pretty clear idea of who I am. Natalie, swimmer, friend, student. It's like all these incarnations have very specific personalities. I don't think there's anyone out there that knows all of them, and if they were morphed together, I'm not sure it would make one Natalie.

Mitch was there last night with Holly, who looked stunning by the way. I don't know how you two left things, but paparazzi were all over her after the press conference. It didn't seem to fluster her at all though, believe me. Of course, maybe that's Mitch's handiwork. He's totally the hero type. I guess I just figured as a clinical psychologist who now works for the military, he'd be sitting at a desk somewhere with burly men of little words. Not crashing Los Angeles hotspots handicapping the latest Hollywood true crime.

Anyway, people still have no clue where you are, which is good. I'll be back around the

Dunes this week if you feel like chatting or not, that's fine too.

Best,

Natalie

———

MORNING WAS the best at the beach house. Not that I'd been getting up before noon lately, but I still remembered you couldn't escape the sun even if the curtains were drawn. Back in Buffalo at this time of year, it was dark by 4:30. Not that I didn't have a soft spot for Western NY, but sometimes I wondered if our lack of winter daylight would turn everyone who lived there into vampires. Or at the very least Vitamin D deficient.

From my perch on the living room couch, I surveyed the remnants of last night's afterparty. Empty glasses, crumpled napkins, a path of sand tracked in from the waterfront through the sliding glass door. Even a surfboard in the middle of the kitchen floor. It impressed me, this carnage was in the hands of a completely sober crowd. I could only imagine what kind of hellscape this place would be if we all partied like we did before our time at the Dunes.

I sat curled up in my blue and orange Pepperdine sweats, one leg tucked beneath me, staring into a mug of coffee that had long gone cold. The caffeine wasn't helping. My thoughts were still tangled in the events of the night before. So many people, all there to do good. Still, it was low-key something I endured instead of enjoyed. The type of thing that I would mark myself "safe" from on social media. The crowd, the chaos...and of course Mitch's unexpected pop-in with his pretty little accessory on his arm.

Across the room, Staci stood at the kitchen counter, scrolling through her phone while simultaneously pouring herself a glass of orange juice. She was already dressed in her standard "work from home" gear, tailored black athleisure, with her long red hair slicked back into a flawless ponytail. No worse for wear after ring-leading the PR circus the night before.

"You're overthinking again," she said without looking up, her voice carrying that no-nonsense tone she'd perfected over the past few years.

I blinked, startled. "What?"

"You've been staring at your coffee for ten minutes," she replied, finally glancing over at me. "Whatever it is, let it go. Last night went well. From what I'm seeing, the whole world thinks you're pretty awesome."

I went through a mental roll call of what she considered "the whole world." All the people who were there last night. My Pepperdine teammates, my friends. Eero, because as my boyfriend, he was obligated. I didn't really know what I did that was so great either. Threw a party and asked people to toss a few bucks my way for charity? Not spectacular. Either way Staci had been doing a pretty good one-woman job of throwing the thing together. She'd made connections everywhere. Sports media, even companies looking for celebrity endorsers. I couldn't believe how many people she'd corralled at that party. And then of course, there were the few uninviteds, who I had no idea where they stood and why the hell they had shown up at all.

"Did you know Mitch was going to be there last night?" I asked.

Staci tilted her head and thoughtfully licked the juice from her lips. "He knew it was happening. He didn't say he was coming, but I didn't tell him not to. And he called me, by the way. I didn't reach out to him."

"Why are you talking to him at all?"

Staci shook her head. "Okay, I'm sorry."

Ari appeared from the hallway, her hair still damp from a shower and her face makeup-free, which somehow only made her look more radiant. She wore an oversized sweatshirt and a pair of leggings, clearly not in any rush to start the day.

"Morning," she said, grabbing a banana from the counter and flopping onto the armchair beside me. She looked at the both of us and chuckled. "So, I walked in on something, didn't I?"

"We were just talking about men," Staci covered. "You know, Lance, Eero..."

"Ahh, and of course Mitch and that bombshell he showed up with last night?" Ari quipped.

This was a path I'd rather not go down. Both talking about Mitch but more so acknowledging the hotness of his date. I looked to Staci to back me up. Fortunately, she picked up on my stink eye. "We don't talk about Mitch anymore around here. Sore subject."

"Sorry. I didn't realize how much I miss when I'm working." Ari peeled her banana slowly then snapped off the top. "Eero seems like a nice guy though. Tall, dark, and handsome. I love a man with an accent. Very mysterious. He swims with you at school, right?"

"Yeah, he's from Spain," I said. "On the Spanish National team."

"Wow so everyone has a man but me," she kidded with a full mouth. "Even our girl Cassidy with Onion Boy."

"Lance and I arranged to be her caregivers for the week," Staci said. "I'm wondering how she would do here instead of the group home."

I couldn't help but smile. Cassidy as a roommate was possibly the most hilarious and unbelievable experience I'd had at the Dunes. Nothing like living with a girl who thinks she stars in her own sitcom.

"You okay, Natalie?" Staci asked, her tone softer now as she studied me.

"Just tired," I said, lifting my cold coffee as if to prove it.

Ari raised an eyebrow but didn't push. "Well, you definitely looked incredible last night," she said instead. "I mean, seriously, that dress? Eero couldn't keep his eyes off you."

Staci grinned. "Neither could half the room. Which is one of the reasons why we're trending," she said matter-of-factly, scrolling through her feed.

"Great," I muttered. "So, what's the verdict?"

Staci smirked. "Mixed bag, as expected. People are either calling it the most inspiring tribute to friendship or wondering if it's just a PR stunt. I think we were genius to make the big auction on Valentine's Day. Really drive home the theme of love."

"PR stunt?" I repeated. "How? What purpose would I have to do that?"

Ari rolled her eyes. "Come on, even I know how much people are dying for you to make a comeback to competitive swimming."

"That's never going to happen," I insisted. If they only knew how fucking ridiculous the suggestion was.

"That's the thing," Ari said. "You're a public figure now. Swimming is just how you got there."

I set my coffee mug down a little harder than necessary. It wasn't that I hadn't ever thought about swimming for real again, but I didn't feel the same ambition that I did before. Maybe it was because Annie wasn't around. But then, there were other things. Anxieties. Fears. All these new dark and gnarled feelings, or old ones no longer dulled by the drugs. Tillie wanted to talk about it in therapy, but it never felt like something I could articulate. I felt like a bucket filling with all this emotion and uncertainty. I lived in constant anticipation of it all spilling over...

"Earth to Natalie?"

...and crashing out.

"What?" I stammered.

"You're not listening to a word any of us are saying, are you?"

I wasn't. It wasn't intentional, but on another level (a more honest one) it was very intentional. Since leaving the Dunes, I'd gotten really good at being "not there" when I needed a break from something that I couldn't physically remove myself from. I think this talent is what made me relatively unaffected by the whole Rapey Racer thing...

"You're doing that thing with your wrist again," Staci said. "It finally healed up. Don't pick the scab."

I looked down at my left hand at the new pink skin attempting to grow back over the area I'd inexplicably rubbed raw. I think it started as a bug bite or an allergy, but I wasn't sure. I pulled the sleeve of my sweatshirt back over my hand.

"Okay, but listen to this," Staci digressed. She scrolled through her phone and cleared her throat. "'Natalie Collins' partnership with Staci Blinkin and Lance Bates is an inspiring and noble endeavor honoring Annie Madsen, but questions remain: Two popular ones. Would an Olympic comeback be out of the question? And what exactly is her connection to the

Damian Cross murder? Speculation is rampant thanks to Holly Inez's attendance at the launch.'"

"Wow," Ari said, dropping her banana peel in her lap. "That's...backhanded."

Staci shrugged. "Honestly, it's not bad. People are paying attention, which is what we need. And not all the coverage is skeptical. Look—this one's from *Sports Today*: 'Collins returns to the public eye as a former addict and abuse survivor, positioning her philanthropic work as a step toward restoring her legacy.'"

"See?" Ari said, pointing at Staci. "There's your silver lining."

The click of a bedroom door opening cut through the room. Cassidy strolled in wearing her pink flannel pajamas but barefoot and carrying a half-eaten bagel in one hand. Her ashy blonde hair was piled in a lopsided bun and the eye makeup from the night before stuck in dark streaks below her sleepy eyes.

"Well, Kev's officially gone," she announced, flopping onto the couch next to me.

"So is his family driving all the way out here from Arizona to get him?" I asked.

"Yeah, he refused to fly and wanted to take a boat instead." She shook her head. "I should have never let him binge watch a whole season of Below Deck."

We collectively bit our lips to stifle the laugher.

I patted her shoulder. "We're sorry he's leaving Cass, but your aunt agreed you could stay with us for the rest of the week. Maybe we can all help you get your mind off of him."

"I just hope he'll be happy at home." Cassidy's hazel eyes narrowed, scanning us with the precision of someone who always knew when something was up. "Why does everyone look sad in here? Were we talking about Mitch or something?"

I stiffened.

Freaking Cassidy.

"No, we were not talking about Mitch," I told her matter-of-factly.

"Yeah right," she said. "Let me guess. You saw him last night with that sexy looking girl and now you're super jealous. Am I close?"

Normally Cassidy's drug-fried filter was one of my favorite things about her, but not in this instance. "No, you are not close."

"Liar." Cassidy leaned back, tossing her bagel onto the coffee table like a grenade. "You know what, if we were Real Housewives, we'd be talking about it. They solve real life problems between every commercial."

"Please tell me we do not resemble in any way the whiny hags on any of those shows," Ari warned.

"Okay, I won't but can we at least talk about what Mitch posted about you?"

"Posted about me? What are you talking about?" I asked warily.

Staci sighed. "I saw it this morning, too." She held up her phone to show me the screen. "Mitch isn't one for social media, but he probably figured he was doing your foundation a favor by putting it out there."

"Put what out there?" I took the phone from her hand. The caption read, "Beauty in the Struggle" and a picture of me from the night before, one I had no idea he took, standing on the patio smiling at something.

I felt my stomach lurch. In my mind's eye, I imagined the way he'd look at me with that strong sincerity of his that grounded and terrified me all at once. I could smell his musky cologne and feel his sandy blond hair slip through my fingers...

"Doesn't seem fair that Holly Inez is running around LA in

party mode while her supposed bestie is at large hiding from a potential murder charge," Ari added. "Unless Holly has something to do with offing Damian Cross, too."

"So much drama! Murder, love, jealousy, betrayal!" Cassidy dramatically pointed her remote at us and pressed "pause" before throwing her head back on the pillow and closing her eyes. "Excuse me, but I just need a moment to process."

The rest of the weekend I spent my time watching "Love at First Sight" with Cassidy, while pretending the trajectory of my life wasn't speeding forward like a freight train. I couldn't sleep Sunday night so since I was up at 4am, I decided I'd make use of my insomnia and head to the pool.

People were genuinely amazed to see me up before the sun at Pepperdine University swim practice. Full disclosure, I actually hadn't been in the water for a while. It was winter break, and I was looking forward to the time off. The fall semester was rough, and I was feeling sort of motivated (guilty) that I should at least try to keep up the appearance of a confident swimmer with my head in the proverbial game.

So, there I was, gripping the edge of the pool, inhaling the humid air. The scent of chlorine, usually a comfort wasn't so much lately. My swim cap felt too tight, and my goggles sucked my eyeballs so hard that my cheeks hurt. The rhythmic splashes around me and the anticipation of Coach Mathews' sharp whistle made me tense. Even the water temp and texture felt off.

"Hey, Natalie, you spacing out?" Janessa's voice broke through my spiraling thoughts. I turned to see her hanging onto the lane divider beside me, water streaming off her cap. Her goggles hid her perpetually kind dark brown eyes, but I could still read her concern. "You okay?"

"Yeah, fine," I said quickly, forcing a smile. "Just…thinking."

Janessa didn't look convinced but didn't press. In the two years we'd been teammates, we could read each other's moods without effort. She simply nodded and jerked her chin toward the far end of the pool where Paris was flipping into another turn. "Paris is crushing it today. I think she's gunning for your spot in the medley relay."

I let out a weak laugh. "She's all about not-so-friendly competition, huh?"

"She came to the party Saturday. That was nice enough of her," Janessa said, splashing water at me.

Before I could respond, the sharp blast of Coach Williams' whistle cut through the air. "Collins, Peters, lane six for sprints! Let's go!"

As Janessa and I lined up at the edge of the pool, Paris swam up beside us, her usual cocky smirk firmly in place. "Ready to eat my wake, Collins?" she teased, adjusting her goggles.

"Only if you can keep it in front of me," I shot back, forcing a grin. Trash talk was just part of the dynamic, but today, it felt heavier, like everything else.

"All right, ladies, focus up," Coach Mathews barked. "Three sprints, a hundred yards. Show me who wants it more."

The whistle blew, and I dove in, the water slicing past me as I powered through the first lap. For those brief moments, there was nothing but the rhythm of my strokes, the burn in my muscles, and the drive to reach the wall first. By the third sprint, my arms felt like lead, and Paris was pulling ahead. She touched the wall a split second before me, surfacing with a triumphant whoop. "Told you," she said, grinning as she flicked water in my direction.

"Don't get used to it," I muttered, pulling myself out of the pool. My chest heaved as I grabbed a towel, trying to steady my breathing.

"Might not happen if you show up to practice more often," Coach Mathews said and scribbled something on his clipboard. "If you want to swim IM, you gotta bone up on Butterfly."

I nodded, biting back the frustration that bubbled in my gut.

"Can't be the best at everything, now can we, It Girl?" Paris taunted and headed for the locker room.

And then, as if on cue, Eero made his way into the natatorium. Men's practice was after the women's, so our ships passed on days like these when we ran over. Paris stood by the doors toweling herself off. She ripped off her swim cap and raked her fingers through her long platinum blonde hair. If I were the jealous type, I might have minded the eyes she made at Eero and the way she flashed a smile as he walked by. I could have also taken issue with the wink he gave her in response.

"Eero and I were talking about you earlier." Janessa took a coyish gulp from her water bottle. "He's got charm, I'll give you that."

"Please don't tell me you're playing relationship counselor again. I get enough of that from Tillie and Staci."

"He's thinking of training for the Olympics. He says you inspire him."

I was flattered. It also surprised me that he was capable of the feeling in the first place. In fact, his lightness was maybe his most appealing quality to me. All charm, no pressure. No risk, all reward. It was easy to be with him. My thoughts never dipped below the emotional surface. He never asked me to go deep, and I never had to. I didn't spiral or second-guess. He was a fun distraction, and maybe that was the whole point.

"I think he wants to take you away for the weekend," Janessa admitted. "Big Bear."

"Take me away? What do you mean, like kidnap me?" I laughed but the alarm I felt was serious for some reason.

"He wants to surprise you. He thinks you could use a weekend; just the two of you."

I blew out a breath, focusing on drying off and trying to ignore the panic I felt simmering inside me. But it's not like I didn't see it coming. I'd been putting off this getaway he'd been hinting at for weeks and I couldn't quite figure out why.

"I can't afford the time away," I stammered. "I have to practice, and I've been at the Dunes mentoring a lot more..."

Janessa laughed and slowly shook her head. "God, you're a good bullshit artist."

"No bullshit," I lied. "I really have a lot going on."

Janessa folded her arms against herself and dramatically gave me a once-over. I sensed what was coming. We both had a mind and a mouth to tell people exactly how we felt about them. I liked our existence that way. No offense given, none taken.

"What?" I asked, ready for what she had to say.

"Eero is a good guy and it's girls like Paris who are waiting to snatch him up if you leave him unattended too long."

"If he's interested in Paris, that seems like a 'him' problem. Not mine."

"That's the thing," she said simply. "I think there *is* a 'you' problem, and I'm sensing it's something you need help with and you don't want anyone to know about it."

Eero strolled over to Janessa and me. He kissed my cheek and handed me a towel from my bag. "Hey baby, how was practice?"

"Not bad. Still kind of recovering from the weekend."

"I figured." He looked back and forth between Janessa and me. Like he knew he'd walked into the middle of something but didn't care what it was. "Maybe we should think about how we can relax later," he said. "You know, just you and me. I'm leaving for that men's swim camp at Berkley next week and I'd like to spend time with you."

The inflection in his voice dripped seduction. Maybe it was his European accent. I didn't hate it, but at the same time, it scared the hell out of me. "Sure," I managed. "I'm sure we could figure something out."

"Perfect. How about we game plan more later? I want to talk to the trainer about my shoulder before I get in the pool."

"That arm giving you trouble?" Paris cooed as she reappeared for no reason. "I couldn't help but overhear. Maybe what you need is a good massage."

Eero politely shrugged her off. Clearly this was a move to rattle my cage, not so much a pass at him. She would have to try harder. It seemed more pathetic than aggressive.

"Don't you get dehydrated from all that drooling?" Janessa eyed Paris. "You think the guys can't tell when a girl is trying as hard as you are?"

"Hey Collins!" Coach Mathews stood in the open door of the swim office, arms crossed, expression unreadable. "Need a word with you. Now."

A cold knot twisted in my stomach. Mathews wasn't one for meetings or talking period. He was more of a barking orders type. I followed him into the small space, the air inside thick with the smell of chlorine. He sat down at his desk, and I sat across. No pleasantries. No time wasted.

"You know why I called you in here?" he asked.

"Should I?"

"Look, we both know you've been in some kind of slump. I'm hoping you can figure it out while you're on break."

I nodded. "Yeah, I thought I'd relax a little before next semester..."

"That's not what I mean." He opened an orange folder on

the desk with the school logo on the front, pulled out a paper and slid it to me. "This was in my school mailbox this morning. You've been placed on academic probation."

The words hit like a slap. "Wait, what?" I stared at him, hoping I'd misheard.

"Effective immediately." He sighed, rubbing a hand over his face. "Your GPA dropped below the university's eligibility requirements. Until you bring it up, you're benched. You can't practice with the team."

It wasn't like I didn't know it was coming. I knew the rules. But the letter I now held in my hands looked very official. Like it was an extra level of serious if they went to the trouble of sending a paper copy.

Coach Matthews softened, just a little. "Look, I know this isn't what you wanted to hear, but it's not permanent. You fix this, and you're back in the water. But right now, my hands are tied."

I nodded stiffly. "Got it."

"Good. Because I need you in the pool, Collins. But I also need you eligible."

As I left the office in a daze, the sound of my teammates laughing and splashing felt miles away. Eero was the center of the circle of them all. Totally carefree and oblivious. There was a part of me that wanted to call him over, tell him so I could share the burden of this news. But then again, maybe it was better something I kept to myself. Too many people knowing too many things made situations hard to control.

THREE

THE DUNES WAS UNUSUALLY quiet for a Wednesday morning. Sunlight streamed through the wide windows and caught on the edges of the framed photos lining the hallways. Each picture was a moment frozen in time. Smiling groups of residents on beach cleanups, art projects, or service days. They were reminders of why I liked it. I fit here. Performance wasn't a condition. Well, at least my failing grades and slow times in the pool didn't exclude me from being useful.

I carried two mugs of herbal tea into the activity room, where Marradine was already seated in her usual spot by the window. She was curled up in an oversized armchair, her knees tucked to her chest as she stared out at the desert. The way her shoulder-length auburn hair caught the light reminded me of the child star she used to be. Way younger than the twenty-two years she was now.

"Hey," I greeted softly, placing one of the mugs on the small table beside her chair. "Thought you might want something warm."

Marradine didn't respond, but her light eyes flicked to the mug for a second before returning to the window. That was progress, at least. In the few weeks I'd been mentoring her, "progress" was measured in small victories. A glance. A nod. Sometimes a faint smile.

"I saw they added peppermint tea to the stash," I continued, taking the seat in a matching chair across from her. "Figured I'd give it a try. Not bad, I'm more of a ginger type of gal."

Nothing. Just the soft sound of the spa music they piped low twenty-four seven and the distant chatter from another room. I leaned back, letting our silence settle. With Marradine, pushing too hard never worked. She needed space, and I'd learned to respect that. But that didn't stop me from trying to reach her in other ways.

"You know," I said after a moment, "I was thinking the other day of that first show you did when you were really young. What was it called? Marradine's Corner? That one where you had your own YouTube channel, and you'd give advice to your Middle School. Anyway, every Saturday morning my brother and I would fight over the remote to make sure we didn't miss it. You were hilarious."

Her fingers twitched against the armrest. A barely noticeable reaction, but at least I knew I was getting through. This strange rhythm we'd fallen into, me talking, her listening...I was cool with it. I could wait. What I wasn't cool with was her being blindsided by trouble brewing outside in the real world, where in here, someone could easily give her a heads up. I still thought about how if someone had warned me about the Racer thing, maybe I would have handled it better.

So, I cleared my throat, pushed our teacups aside, and leaned across the little coffee table to look her dead in the eye. "Listen Marradine, I want you to know something that I'm not sure how you're gonna feel about, but I want to tell you all the same."

No reaction, but I still forged ahead.

"Over the weekend, there was a big press conference about Damian Cross. His death was officially ruled a murder and people think you're in hiding because you either did it or know who did."

Still no reaction.

"I know you were brought here because there were all sorts of drugs in your system when they found you passed out in his barn. But I'm thinking you might be the person to fill in some of the blanks as far as what went down that night. If you could... and if you wanted to."

Her eyes shifted to me, holding my gaze for just a second before drifting back to the window. Still no words, but I could see the faintest flicker of acknowledgment.

"It's funny," I said, picking up my mug and staring thoughtfully in it. "Does it ever piss you off when strangers act like they know you? Like just because they see your face on a screen, they know your whole life?" I hesitated, choosing my words carefully. "I know how much pressure that must have been. How hard it must have been to be perfect all the time."

What was I yammering about? Was I making this about me? She swiveled the chair toward me but just blinked at me, her chin resting on her knees.

"You can tell me stuff, Marradine. Seriously."

Before I could say more, the door creaked open, and Tillie, head counselor of the Dunes and dear friend of mine, poked her head in.

"Hey, Nat," she said, her voice hushed. "Can I steal you for a minute? There's an issue at reception we need your help with."

I glanced at Marradine, reluctant to leave, but Tillie's expression told me it couldn't wait. "I'll be right back," I told her.

The instant I stepped into the lobby, I knew something was

wrong. The soft voices and the quiet calm I always associated with this place was drowned out by an ominous buzz. When I rounded the corner to the reception, the noise was full-on deafening. There they were: a wall of reporters, about twenty or so deep crowding the front desk, with cameras slung over their shoulders, microphones clutched like weapons, and wide eyes demanding loudly to be heard.

Now!

Shit.

"Hey! That's Natalie Collins!" someone shouted, and every head swiveled toward me.

At first there was a weird pause. Like their collective mind realized who I was and wondered why the hell I was there. And then, madness. The mob barreled toward me and surrounded me in a circle.

"We're just here to ask a few questions!" some bald guy in a wrinkled suit insisted. "Does Marradine Addison have a statement yet in the murder of Damian Cross? Does she know if she'll be arrested?"

Tillie pushed between them and me in her white Dune staff golf shirt holding her hands in the air like she was directing traffic. "Information about anyone in attendance here is strictly confidential," she shouted at him.

"In attendance?" he repeated with a snarky raised brow. "So, does that mean she won't be taken into custody? Has she retained an attorney?"

Everyone was screaming at once now. All variations of the same questions. I realized that even staff members had ventured closer to hang around in earshot of this exchange. Usually, Dunes staff weren't ones impressed by celebrities. I could attest to that firsthand from when I was a resident here. But this was the hottest Hollywood murder case since OJ Simpson in the 90's. Everyone was a Lookie-Loo now.

"What's your connection to the victim, Natalie?" Some guy in a Dodgers cap yelled from the back. "Were you at Damian Cross' party that night, too?"

The photographers were like vultures circling a fresh carcass. Their rumpled shirts and worn jeans seemed like afterthoughts, as if appearances didn't matter as long as they could get the shot. I hated the smugness in their eyes, the way their expressions teetered between calculated indifference and snide satisfaction, as though they already knew they'd caught me in some damning moment.

I stepped forward, my heart pounding. "Sorry to disappoint you but I'm here on a social call. I'm straight, happily on the proverbial wagon."

"How do you know Marradine Addison?" Some pixy-cut blonde girl in a Nike track suit shouted. "What is your perception of her and Damian Cross' relationship?"

"You guys know I mentor here," I said with the fakest ass smile only Staci would appreciate. "If you read the press release I issued last week, you'd know that. I don't have any connections, opinions, or judgments."

"Please, that's not the little hothead Natalie Collins we know!" Some older man quipped and the rest of them chuckled.

Asshole.

"You all know this is private property, right?" I snapped. "And no one is gonna give you any information about residents here."

"Are you keeping secrets for her, Natalie?"

"Are you a resident, Natalie? Is that how you know her?"

"Natalie Collins, Do YOU have something to do with the murder of Damian Cross?"

Fucking Bald Guy. He trumped his trashy constituents with an obvious accusation in his question. For a moment, the mob hesitated. It was only a breath, but I felt it. A sliver of control in the chaos. Everyone waited for what would emerge from my dry mouth.

"Natalie," he coaxed, his tone syrupy and false, "you must understand, the public has questions. They deserve answers."

"I had nothing to do with Damian Cross."

"But you're here with Marradine and don't seem happy to be recognized for it. I thought you were proud of your outreach here. Are you hiding something because you're afraid this might affect your own legal drama currently unfolding back in Buffalo?

I forced my jaw not to clench. I'd been through this too many times, and I knew exactly what he was doing. Dangling the carrot. Trying to make me jump for it. "What is it with you people? You think getting in someone's face will inspire them to tell you anything? What's going on in Buffalo is over. Old news."

Had I underestimated people's disgusting interest in such a fucked-up story? Especially one clear across the country? Tillie now stood at the reception desk, her expression blank. Tillie has been my counselor since the first dark days when I got here. As far as I could tell, she had no idea what the reporter was talking about, and I wanted to keep it that way. This could not get out of control. Not here. Not like this.

"Natalie, all we want is just a few words!"

"Oh, I've got a few words for you," I snapped. "Two actually. F..."

"That's enough," Tillie cut in, stepping between us. Her voice was calm but laced with steel. "This is private property, and you're trespassing. The police are on their way in and will arrest you if you don't leave immediately."

The reporter hesitated, clearly weighing his options. Finally, he let out a frustrated huff and started backing toward the door with the crowd. "This isn't over," he said, pointing a finger at me. "The public deserves the truth, Ms. Collins. Don't forget that."

As soon as he was gone, I let out a held breath. "How did he even find out I was here?"

"No idea. But we'll figure it out. Now, let's make sure Marradine doesn't catch wind of this. The last thing she needs is to feel like she's under a microscope."

I nodded, my thoughts racing. This was exactly what I didn't want, to have my time at the Dunes turned into a spectacle. When I returned to the activity room, Marradine was gone. My heart sank. Had she overheard? Had the chaos scared her off? But then I spotted the mug of tea on the table, now empty, and a folded piece of paper beside it.

I picked up the note, my pulse quickening as I unfolded it. The handwriting was small and shaky, like she hadn't used a pen in years. But it was unmistakably hers.

Thank you for remembering me.

———

That night Staci, Janessa, Cassidy, Ari and I hung out on the deck of the beach house with a table full of junk food and a vast selection of fruity mocktails made from recipes we found on Instagram. Our earnest attempts at "adulting" did not allow us a lot of opportunity for late night mid-week hangs lately. Tonight though, the shitshow at the Dunes provided exception.

Recently, my insomnia mostly made me too tired to socialize in the daytime. It was nice to know my growing disfunction had some sort of warped payoff because it was 1 a.m. and I was wide awake. We sat in a circle around the fire pit, huddled in blankets with our hoodies pulled up and tied tight around us. A string of fairy lights dangled over the wooden deck, lighting the space enough where we could see each other, but dark enough to keep the bugs away. Lance popped in after a late showing at the gallery. He cuddled up next to Staci in their shared Snuggie. The gang was all there and that didn't happen much anymore.

Well, almost the whole gang.

"Hey, don't you guys have swim practice at 7 a.m.?" Staci asked Janessa and me, like she suddenly realized where we were and what time it was. She looked at her watch. "How could you possibly stay afloat with so little sleep?"

Janessa stifled a yawn and stretched. "It's fine. Late practice tomorrow for me. I'm taking advantage of winter break."

"Same," I covered.

"Looks like Cassidy is all partied out." Janessa nodded to a blanket-covered lump passed out on a chaise lounge clutching a bowl of popcorn in one hand and her remote in the other.

Staci smiled and reached over to tuck the blanket around her. "She's comfortable here," she said. "I'm wondering if it's possible for her to stay around longer."

I'd been thinking that, too. It had been three years since Cassidy was my roommate at the Dunes, and I had to admit having my own room again could get a little lonely. There were times, especially over the past few months, when I thought if Cassidy was around, I wouldn't be so hyper-focused on my own bullshit. Watching out for Cassidy was always the best distraction.

"I wouldn't mind having her here," Ari said, dumping a pile of popcorn from the bag into her plastic bowl. "I didn't realize how much I missed her lack of filter."

Staci took a sip of her pink drink and swallowed thoughtfully. "Cassidy has this rich aunt who's been making a lot of her decisions. Natalie and I have talked to her before. She's kind of mean, but she seems to have Cassidy's best interest at heart."

"It's Cass' money, too," I chimed in. "Remember she's a trust fund baby."

Ari nodded. "Cass already mentioned how she doesn't want to go back to the group home without Kevin. I feel bad sending her there."

"Well, we have a fourth bedroom," Lance said. "And I've already gotten used to the fact that I'm surrounded by women, so it doesn't bother me if she stays."

Janessa laughed. "Clearly, I didn't know her at the Dunes, but she does seem to like it here. She's super heavily invested in the Damian Cross murder trial coverage. The way she talks about it, it sounds like she's been watching just as many conspiracy theory documentaries as that Onion Boy."

"So, you must know the latest updates, Nat." Lance leveled his gaze at me from across the fire. "I mean, now that we all heard about the Dunes new famous resident."

I groaned. "You saw the news, too, huh?"

"Nope." He put his arm around Staci. "My girl here knows more than CNN."

Everyone laughed, including me. Soft spot for Marradine aside, Staci did like a good piece of gossip. "You guys know I couldn't tell you I was seeing her. Confidentiality and all that."

"Does Marradine Addison have a statement yet?" Janessa asked. "I mean, I know she was passed out and all, but does she remember anything about that night?"

"How could she have a statement if she doesn't speak?" I laughed.

"'Doesn't want to' or 'can't?'" Janessa wiggled a brow in suggestion.

"Yeah," Lance added. "What is that about? Like some sort of PTSD or something?"

I topped off my virgin colada from the pitcher beside me and considered the question. The way I saw at it, shit happened to Marradine she didn't feel like discussing. I got that. How come no one else could?

"And what about Holly Inez?" Janessa asked, as she carefully stacked a piece of cheese on a wheat thin. "And that gorgeous blond guy you all know that she came with to the launch party the other night. They all play a part in this somehow, right? Weren't they at the mansion the night of the murder?"

Staci, Lance, and I exchanged a look. Janessa and I had gotten close over the past year since she joined the Pepperdine swim team, but she didn't know hardly anything about Mitch. That was intentional. Me trying to pretend I existed in a world where he didn't. He'd been off at Marine basic training in San Diego, a requirement for his new fancy job, and I'd implemented a policy to keep all bad past juju in a different zip code. Only Staci knew the real history of Mitch and me. Even then, there were parts I'd never told anyone. Leave it to a small world that Mitch somehow was connected to the Damian Cross case, or at least connected to a connection.

"Holly Inez and Mitch are none of my business," I said. "All we know is that Damian Cross was some famous movie producer who was found dead in a horse stall after a private party he hosted. He was strangled. There were over a hundred people there. And Holly could have blown Damian Cross up for all I care, but I don't see Marradine having anything to do with it."

Cassidy sat up at the mention of media coverage on television and dumped her bowl of popcorn to the deck. She wiped the sleep from her eyes and pressed the "unmute" button on her remote. "The Damian Cross case is trending on every social media source and online news service. Everyone loves a Hollywood true crime story."

I let out a slow breath. "Yeah. I noticed. Have a good sleep, Cass?"

· · ·

"Just recharging." She picked a few spilled popcorn kernels off her blanket and thoughtfully popped them in her mouth. "Everybody at that party that night has been interviewed, except Marradine. There are potential suspects but nothing solid. However, most people can say the last time they saw Damian Cross alive, he was heading to the stables with Marradine Addison."

Lance leaned forward, resting his elbows on his knees. "So, you think she actually, like, did it?"

Cassidy shrugged. "Maybe, but why? She's a brat, but she was his new rising star and set to be the lead in his new film."

"Why is Holly Inez involved?" Janessa asked. "She seems too pretty and perfect to be wrapped up in a murder. But then again, she was friends with Marradine the wild child..."

"Damian's business partner is Holly Inez's brother, Brody," Cassidy informed us, reaching for the pretzel bag. "Brody Inez is the former Marine guy who hosts that show American Hero Challenge."

"That's how Mitch met Holly," Staci said. "Mitch was working with Holly's brother and somehow and their paths crossed."

"Brody Inez said in an interview he works with a therapist to make sure he stays natural in his physical training," Lance said. "That sounds like a Mitch thing."

A heavy silence fell over the group. The waves crashed below, from the water's edge, filling the space between our unspoken thoughts.

"Maybe Marradine *thinks* she killed him," Cassidy offered in a quiet voice. "Like she doesn't totally remember because her mind is playing tricks on her. Like a possessed person."

Lance frowned. "What do you mean she doesn't remember?"

Staci rolled her eyes. "The true facts reported by the LAPD

is that Marradine was found blacked out literally with blood on her hands in the stable office."

"So the barn on the property is where all this went down?" Janessa asked. "That's where they found Damian Cross, right?"

Cassidy nodded emphatically. "According to the reports, BUT insiders think that's false and it's some sort of police coverup. No updates. No arrests."

"Wait, what about Holly then?" Ari asked. "And she was at the mansion with Mitch that night. I wonder what he thinks."

My stomach twisted. I *knew* this was where the conversation was headed, but I wasn't ready to say it out loud.

"How serious is it between the two of them, you think?" Ari continued.

Janessa popped another piece of popcorn in her mouth. "Holly and Marradine were buddies. I know she's pretty and all, but Holly Inez doesn't seem like she's smart enough to angle a murder investigation."

"I still don't know how Mitch got tangled up with her," Lance said, shaking his head. "Smart or not, the two just seem like really strange bedfellows."

"Don't say bedfellows," Staci mumbled.

Lance nodded to me. "Sorry, Nat. I didn't mean it that way."

The truth was it made perfect sense for someone like Mitch to be drawn to someone like Holly. It went beyond the obvious to say that he was as drop dead handsome as she was gorgeous. On a more "less shallow" side, Mitch was a helper and do-gooder. And Holly Inez seemed to need all the help she could get at this point to keep her perky tight ass out of jail. If all the reports were true, of course. Who better to keep her on the right path than a boyfriend like Mitch?

Lance rubbed a hand over his face. "So, what are we saying here? That maybe Mitch knows something about Holly and Damian Cross and why Marradine won't speak?"

"Could be," I admitted. "All I know is I can't be concerned about that right now. I just need to focus on getting the foundation going and the auction ready. We're so close now."

"And we don't need you involved in a scandal. It will scare away donors," Staci added.

Lance laughed. "Holly Inez's family has money to spare. She could kick you a few bucks. Although she might be on a budget now if she has to bail herself out of jail."

Everyone laughed but I didn't see the humor. Mitch, school, swimming, the foundation. So many things to consider. A cold gust of wind swept over the deck, sending a chill down my spine. I huddled closer to the fire and stared at it, letting the heat make my eyes water. Or maybe it wasn't so much the fire.

FOUR

THE SANTA MONICA PIER was one of my new indulgences since relocating to the west coast. It was part street fair, part ocean resort with a dash of kitschy nostalgia. I loved the cheesy arcade games where you wacked moles in holes and winged balls at impossible targets. Eero the European loved any innovation of good ol' American sugar delivery. Funnel cakes, cotton candy, and those big candy apples you got near the Route 66 sign on the main walkway.

I walked with Eero as he assessed his selection of Skee-Ball machines. It amused me that even in a setting like this, he dressed for an evening on a yacht. Over the six months or so we'd been together, I'd gotten used to the sophisticated European vibe of his, with the hair product and the shaving twice a day and skin care routine with more steps than the Empire State building. Tonight he wore white shorts with a light blue button-down, his sunglasses resting on his dark head like an accessory instead of a necessity. Very GQ. I stood beside him in a baggy grey t-shirt and cutoffs, the kind of outfit you throw on when you don't want to be seen. Nothing too clingy.

Nothing too revealing. He dressed like he lived in his skin. I dressed like I was borrowing mine.

The lights flashed a little too bright tonight, and the sounds, all those bells and buzzers, seemed louder than usual. But I was fine. Totally fine. I took a deep breath and let it out slowly.

"This one," Eero declared, patting the side of Skee-Ball machine six. "This one is lucky. I can feel it."

I half-laughed. "Oh yeah? How do you know?"

"I *don't* know." He shrugged. "I just got a hunch. And hunches usually go in my favor."

"It's pretty risky to make decisions just based on a vibe."

He studied me and tossed a skee-ball back in forth in his hands. "Speaking of vibes, you seem a little off tonight. You're all right?"

"Of course," I answered quickly. "I had a headache earlier, that's all." I put two fingers on each of my temples and rubbed them slowly to sell my story.

"Do you want to play something else?"

Did I? I scanned the area around me. So many people pushing close. Sharing my space, breathing my air. My vision narrowed and did that weird thing where the edges around it turned black. My heart began to race. There were pinball machines and dart boards. Children ran screaming and people laughed. There was a rhythm to it all—the digital bells, the hiss of the water pistols, and the fucking, relentless, hollow, thumping of the basketball free-throw game:

clang, bounce, clang, bounce, clang.

"Ring!"

I nearly fell to my knees when Eero's Skee-Ball machine exploded with light and sound. High score. Everyone within earshot applauded in appreciation. Except for me, who just stood there like a catatonic freak, digging my fingernails into my fisted palms.

He gave a dramatic sigh and threw up his hands. "That's it. Game over. I've peaked. Might as well retire early," he said.

"I'd hate for you to quit while you're hot," I managed.

He tossed his last ball without looking. It hit the 100-point ring perfectly. He turned to me with a cocky grin. "See? Manifestation."

I wanted to smile back, to meet his energy, to match his mood. Really, I was just trying to keep my head from exploding in public.

This is fine. You're fine. Just lights. Just noise. You're not back there.

"Hey," I said with as strong of a voice I could muster. "You want to head out to the water? Watch the sunset?"

He raised his brow. "Slurpee first?"

"Sure."

He peeled off toward the stand, and I hung back, watching the way he moved. So casual, so at ease, like the world had never given him a reason to flinch. What was that like? I drifted toward the boardwalk railing and watched the sun inch lower on the horizon, a smudge of orange and gold bleeding into the waves. By the time Eero came back with a neon-blue Slurpee in one hand and a cherry red one in the other, I had found a little patch of chill to settle into.

We sat on a weathered bench near the edge of the boardwalk, and he handed me the cherry one. "Sweets for my sweet," he said with a flair like he recognized his cheesiness. I took it and we offered cheers before we both took a sip.

That was the cool thing about Eero; always relaxed. The exact definition of cool. His chillness was the exact opposite of the high anxiety I'd been feeling lately. I tried to ignore it so Eero didn't notice. That usually worked. Eero was too enthralled with living to notice me trying to do the same. "Thanks for the burger earlier by the way," I said between gulps of my drink. "Peanut butter was a surprisingly delicious condiment."

"It's pretty good, right?" He laughed. "Adds extra protein. George from the swim team showed me that trick. You can add an egg, too. Great for hangovers."

"At least that's something I don't have to worry about," I made sure I said it with wit. That was another thing I liked about Eero. He didn't treat me any differently than a person who wasn't in recovery. Then again, he was a huge proponent of the "California Sober" theory. According to popular culture and Demi Lovato, booze and pot were fine as long as it wasn't the poison that inspired your downfall in the first place. This notion was controversial to me. Booze I could take or leave and pot just made me lazy, so why poke the proverbial bear over it? I hadn't had anything since leaving the Dunes. I wanted to keep my flawless streak going.

"Maybe I'll learn to love the American obsession with ranch dressing on everything," he kidded back. "I have to admit it's not bad with American pizza."

"See, you're adapting."

We laughed together and it felt good. This was nice. Low stakes. Sitting and having a conversation about nothing I gave a real shit about with someone who didn't give a shit about anything. I could feel the blood reach my extremities again.

"You know," he said on an exhale. "Dates like this are great, but I miss spending the time we spent in the pool together and being at the gym with you. Now it's like you're always off in your own head."

"I know," I replied. "I just have a lot on my plate."

He laughed. "That's such an American thing to say. And yeah, Love, you do, but you only have as much going on as you allow. How can I get you to follow my lead and enjoy yourself more?" He winked and took a sip of what was left of his Slurpee.

"I do enjoy myself." My fingers played nervously with the hem of my shorts.

Eero's expression softened. "Look, don't take this the wrong way. I wasn't around when your friend Annie was sick or when you were at the Dunes taking care of yourself. But time has moved on. Maybe what you need is to let loose and let some of your past go."

I blinked, then literally bit my lip to the point where I could have drawn blood. I'd noticed the past few months I wasn't as quick tempered as I'd always been. Like my reaction time on comebacks had slowed due to slight indifference. This poke though, I felt it. "But you just told me you wanted me to be in the pool more. Swimming was my past."

"What I'm saying is that life is for the living, Natalie. You can only grieve for so long."

I glanced away, trying not to hold my offense against him. He didn't mean it anyway. Eero wasn't one for deep and meaningful conversation. I was never even sure if he fully understood recovery. He didn't like details or backstory so there was no pressure on me to unload any of my personal drama. Win, win. I snagged his drink since I'd finished mine and took a long mind-freezing gulp.

"Have you been following the news?" I asked, attempting to steer the conversation toward something on our very basic level. "The Damian Cross case—it's all over the headlines again."

"Ah, the murder case," he said with a nonchalant chuckle. "You and Janessa were talking about it the other day, but I wasn't paying that close attention."

"Well, one of the residents I work with at the Dunes is sort of involved with it."

"Don't get wrapped up in someone else's stupid drama,

Natalie. Who cares about that guy? The way I heard it he was a scumbag who had it coming anyway."

"But it's more than that, Eero. And I'm wondering if it's going to affect people I care about."

Eero leaned back, looking up at the night sky as if this whole conversation was boring him to tears. "You worry too much, Nat."

"I'm not worrying. I'm just making observations."

He shook his head. "This is why you freak out. You have so much going on in your brain, it misfires. You say you're so busy, but you clearly have enough time to worry about stupid stuff like celebrity gossip. You let things get to you. Like Paris at the pool."

"Paris?" I repeated, completely blindsided by the mention of her name. "What does she have to do with anything?"

"She's a rival not an enemy. You should be glad she's around to light a fire under you." He turned toward me and took my hand. It was cold from the drink he'd been holding. "I miss that fire in you Natalie."

If this was his version of sincerity, it felt more like a complaint. "I'm working on it," I managed.

"You know what you need? A break. Let's take off this weekend. Drive up to Big Sur or out to Joshua Tree or whatever American national treasure inspires you. Clear your head a little."

I smiled like I meant it, nodding because it was easier than answering.

The waves rolled in, steady and loud. The sun had dipped below the horizon now, and the world was cooling fast. Eero stood and offered me a hand. "Come on, before the parking lot turns into a war zone."

I let him pull me up. We walked in step, his arm brushing mine, easy and light.

I didn't say another word. And thankfully, neither did he.

———

I wandered into the kitchen, still damp from the cool night air and was immediately intercepted by Staci. She was darting around in a red sauce–splattered apron, hair escaping from her messy bun, practically shoving me toward the counter.

"Oh, thank God you're back!" she exclaimed, her tone a mix of relief and urgency. "Just in time to do some dishes."

I stopped in the doorway assessing the smell of burnt cheese and fanning the faint fog of smoke. "What's going on here?"

"Aunt Rose is coming," Lance declared while he balanced on a kitchen bar stool, detaching the smoke detector from the ceiling. "We're testing recipes of all her favorites."

Staci marched over to the center island where a commercial-grade mixer was already set up next to her open laptop. "Cassidy's Aunt Rose is coming Saturday. We need everything to be perfect," she said, her fingers dancing over the keyboard. "And I guarantee there aren't any favorite dishes this woman could possess that would be in a repertoire of mine," Staci insisted.

"I don't know," Cassidy disagreed from the couch. "Your ramen noodles are getting so much better. Not so watery anymore."

"Thanks for noticing."

Cassidy was sprawled out in her Hello Kitty pajamas; a mixing bowl balanced on her lap. In one hand she wielded a wooden spoon, while the other hovered over the TV remote. "Why aren't you helping?" I teased. "This is all for your benefit, you know."

Cassidy scoffed, taking a big, defiant mouthful of cupcake batter. "Are you kidding? I'm doing all the work. Where do you think Staci got all the fancy recipes? I streamed all four seasons of Bake Off." She shoved the batter-covered spoon in her mouth as if daring me to question her methods.

"You do know that batter's got raw eggs, right? You'll get salmonella."

Cassidy shrugged nonchalantly. "I'll take my chances."

Staci dumped her remaining batter into the mixer and hauled dirty dishes toward the sink. "So, how was your night?" she asked, glancing over her shoulder. "You're home early."

"I told him I was tired."

"I call bullshit." Cassidy came to the kitchen and dropped her bowl on the island.

"Something happen with Eero?" Staci asked.

"No," I answered quickly.

Lance stepped back down to the floor and replaced the stool next to the island. Now all three of them studied me closely. I stared at my feet.

"It's not just about being tired, is it?" Staci said. "Something else is up with you."

I wasn't sure if it was simply an observation on Staci's part or an accusation. It wasn't like I was trying to hide anything. The grades would come up, swimming was too exhausting for the moment anyway, plus with the foundation and my work at the Dunes, I needed a breather. I'd adjust and adapt. "You guys think Eero is a nice guy, right?"

"Sure." Staci shrugged. "He's fun. Great to have at a party. I'm thinking of asking him for his recipe for that virgin sangria he made for trivia night a few weeks ago. Maybe Aunt Rose would like it."

"I like him, too," Lance added, taking a slightly burnt cookie off a cooling tray on the stove. "I've gone to the gym with him a few times. He doesn't kick my ass like Mitch does. Way more low-key."

Staci glared at Lance, presumably over the mention of

Mitch's name. It was fine. Lance and Mitch were friends when they were at the Dunes together as residents before Staci and I even knew them. I assumed Lance still hung out with Mitch here and there.

"Yeah, I guess a lot of people like Eero." I thought out loud. "You think he's someone a person can trust?"

Staci raised her brow. "A person, or you?"

Clearly, I'd asked an interesting question because Cassidy pointed her remote at me and pressed "up" on the volume. Staci and Lance gazed up at me with wide eyes. "So what's up," Staci asked and brushed the flour from her hands. "Relationship drama?"

"I'm not even sure we're in a real relationship."

"Why not? What's stopping you?"

For a few seconds I mentally reviewed all the things I'd observed and called into question about who Eero was as a human being. He was cute, but vain at times, smart but not about things that mattered. Like, he could calculate the macros needed for a specific workout in his head, but I had to explain three times to him how to calculate a twenty percent tip at a restaurant when he left his phone in the car. Then there were the little light white lies he told, like adding twenty pounds to what he could actually bench press or "rounding up" his grade on a sociology test. Meaningless but annoying. His mention of Paris didn't bother me. It was the thought that there was something they knew that I didn't that I hated. "Do you think Eero is a player? Like do you think he's got other girls he talks to?"

Staci and Lance shared a look. "We didn't think you were that serious, are you?" Staci asked.

"Well, I'm not seeing anyone else, and I didn't think he was."

"Is that because you're hung up on Mitch?" Cassidy

grabbed a cookie and shoved it in her mouth. "Just saying," she said in between chomps.

"This is nothing to do with Mitch," I insisted.

The sliding glass door opened behind us. Janessa walked in, kicked off her flip flops, and held up a Shop 'n Save bag. "I found everything we need for a bread bowl!"

"Natalie thinks Eero is cheating on her," Cassidy blurted while taking the grocery bag from her hands.

Janessa sat down beside me. "You're kidding! How did you find out?"

"I don't know anything," I insisted. "And I don't think that. I'm just wondering if you guys think he's a loyal person."

Cassidy rolled her eyes. "She's not sleeping with him, so she's wondering if someone else is. She hasn't told us if it's anyone in particular."

I took a deep breath. One of the things Cassidy had been working on in therapy is recognizing the difference between "inside-your-head-thoughts" and "okay-to-say-out-loud-thoughts." Clearly this was still a grey area to her. "Cass, sex doesn't have anything to do with this," I reminded her.

She popped open a can of cola she pulled from Janessa's bag. "That's my point."

"Tonight, when I was with Eero at the pier he mentioned Paris and it made me think of the other day at the pool how they seemed kind of friendly," I admitted. "I just thought it was weird."

Janessa didn't seem surprised at the mention of Paris' name. She chuckled slightly and shook her head. "That bitch just likes to cause trouble, doesn't she?"

"So you think it's possible," Staci asked.

Janessa shrugged. "Anything's possible. I just don't think Eero would go for it. Paris has her own agenda."

"It sounds like to me, you're gaslighting yourself," Cassidy pointed at me with a carrot stick as if she meant business. "I saw a discussion about that just the other day on the Kelly Clarkson show. It's like talking yourself out of a good relationship."

"It's not gaslighting if you're taking note of your own observations," I told her.

"Then you're just being paranoid," Cassidy replied. "I get that way when I watch too much true crime."

The truth was I was never a trusting person and I was beginning to wonder if seeing things through a sober lens made it that much worse. Like everything was hyper-focused now.

"Hasn't Eero been asking you for a weekend getaway?" Lance asked.

"Yeah…"

"Maybe you should go," Staci suggested. "Might be fun and less stressful with a change of scenery."

"Maybe." I dragged my finger through the batter bowl sitting in front of us on the counter and stuck it in my mouth. Salmonella be damned.

"Speaking of out of town, another letter from your mom came today in the snail mail." Lance pointed to the haphazard pile of flyers and envelopes stacked on the counter by the kitchen door. "She's sent you more shit the past two months than she has the past two years. What gives?"

I went to the stack of mail with a practiced indifference, like someone who didn't care about the answers they already knew. Bills, an invitation to some art event, junk mail, all I tossed aside until my fingers found the letter. Not one from my mother, but from the University. My heart sank as I recognized the orange and purple crest glaring up at me from the envelope, as if daring me to open it in front of everyone.

"Your mom's been busy," Lance joked, oblivious as he grabbed a glass of water. I forced a laugh that I hoped sounded casual.

"Yeah, she's just catching up, I guess," I muttered, tearing open the envelope at a deliberate pace. My eyes darted across the text, searching for the words I'd been dreading. *Failure. Expulsion. Reapply...*

For a moment, the words swirled and coalesced into something larger than I could process. My chest tightened, but I kept my face perfectly blank. Years of swimming had taught me game face. This was no different. I folded the letter neatly, slipping it back into the envelope as casually as I could, all the while feeling the weight of it pressing down on me.

"Bad news?" Staci asked, not bothering to look up as she scraped batter into a cake pan.

"Not really," I lied with a shrug, my voice steady, detached. I waved the torn envelope in the air. "Just school stuff."

Cassidy went back to the couch and flopped down with a nod. "I'm surprised you could even stay awake to go to class. Do you ever sleep anymore? I hear you up during the night, God knows what you're doing."

"And why are you awake in the middle of the night to hear me?" I shoved the envelope into my hoodie pocket before anyone could press further, hoping the humor would deflect their attention.

But Janessa's eyes lingered on me for a second longer than the rest. "You're okay, though?" she asked, softer than I expected.

"Totally," I said quickly, too quickly. "Anyway, what's the plan for this kitchen disaster? Need another set of hands?"

Staci shoved a whisk into my hand and launched into a monologue about the perfect size cookies while Cassidy resumed licking batter from her fingers. I let their voices wash over me. Inside, I could feel the panic clawing at the edges of my resolve, but I kept my shit together. I could fall apart later when no one was looking.

FIVE

Dear Marradine
January 5, 11:08 p.m.

So just checking in. I didn't want you to think I'd forgotten about you. I hope you're sleeping well. Dunes' mattresses are surprisingly comfortable. The food isn't bad either. Late night desserts are pretty good. You should take advantage of their fudge brownies. I'm not even a chocolate person and I love them.

I'm so sorry about that big scene in the lobby of the Dunes last week. I'm not sure what you saw or heard of it, but at least the security staff got rid of them pretty quick. I feel like you would understand about paparazzi and obnoxious journalists better than anyone else. But man are they mean. They construct their own narratives about a person and sell it hard no matter how inaccurate they are. That's the thing about being in the spotlight. You have no space to be you. Sure, it's great when you win a race, or in your case, release a movie but...it doesn't seem like the victories are as much of a big deal as the failures. I guess that's human nature, right? The biggest reason why some people like to build others up is to tear them down in the end. That sounds so bitter. Even I can hear it in my own voice. Someone told me once that bitterness is a sign of a person running scared.

Is it ironic that I don't talk to that person anymore?

I can't blame you for wanting to keep your mouth shut these days. I don't feel like communicating with anyone much myself. More and more, I'm feeling like anytime I open myself up to anyone, it's just an opportunity for them to hurt me. Or they have an ulterior motive. I realize that sounds paranoid, but I'd like to think it's self-preservation. If I'm going to make the right choices in life, I have to make sure they're well strategized. No one's ever faulted me for my sport psychology. It's out of the pool I've been called a mental train wreck...

———

I JOLTED AWAKE, my laptop sliding off its perch on my stomach and landing on the floor with a dull thud. Great. I scooped it up, half-prepared to mourn its loss, but the screen was still lit. I wiped the half-sleep from my eyes and squinted at the open document. Just scattered thoughts, unfinished sentences. And then there were the random tabs I had open. An Alaskan cruise website, some link to cat adoption services. And then there was the last search prompt before I dozed off... "college dropout glow-up stories that aren't lies."

My pink digital clock by my bed said 3:37. I attempted mental math, figuring both how long I'd been out and how much more sleep I would need to function as a human being in the morning. At least there was no swim practice to be rested for anymore. Probably for the best because my new nocturnal bull-shit was wearing me out.

A dark room. Cool. Like, the temperature was not warm. I've always had this thing about burrowing into my bed covers. In fact, since I was a kid, I took great pride in sleeping in what I liked to call a "bed burrito." That's when you tuck all your sheets and blankets in really tight so you have to slide in from the top instead of pulling all your covers over you. When I first got to the beach house, I made the bed the same way because as it turns out, southern California nights are remarkably cool, but sometimes I would overheat like a broken furnace. At least that's what it felt like. Waking up soaking wet, with a racing heart and parched mouth fighting the urge to run screaming outside.

Lately they'd gotten so bad, I was starting to dread falling asleep at night. I felt like a toddler fighting myself over my own bedtime. The only way I could trick my brain was to have one leg exposed and hanging off the edge of the bed. Just in case I had to wake up quick to make a getaway.

Tonight I would resort to a variation of this new fucked up ritual of mine. I stood at the foot of my bed and did a three-sixty spin with my arms outstretched. I had no idea why I started doing this. My best guess is that I liked knowing I was alone in the space. This was when I'd notice every sound around me was magnified. The hum of my computer's fan, the faint drip of my bathroom faucet, the distant groan of the air conditioner kicking back on. I could smell things, too. Salt air, even popcorn, if Staci made some the evening earlier.

After a moment of just standing there, I would lament my next move. Changing my sheets. Replacing the tangled, sweat-stained covers with fresh, crisp linens. This sounds dramatic, and it felt dramatic, but the relief I felt when I slipped the last corner of the fitted sheet over the mattress edge was like releasing a deeply held breath. I'd smooth it out, letting the heat of the friction tickle my palm and breathe in the fabric softener the motion would kick up. I'd finish the job, perfectly aligning the pillowcase seams with the pillow and place it directly in the middle of the bed against the headboard. This felt decadent. A secret indulgent like a second piece of cake no one saw you take (this is a Tillie analogy).

As I did this, I mentally berated myself for not only giving in to my stupid intrusive thoughts (more Tillie speak), but for wasting detergent and water. The thing was, those crisp, clean linens felt like a safe haven, a physical reminder that, at least in that moment, nothing had to be carried over from yesterday if I didn't want it to be.

I reached for the small bottle of lavender spray on my nightstand and misted my pillowcase. Ari was big into aroma therapy and kept a bunch of bottles and diffusers in her room. Lavender was my favorite from her collection. It somehow made the darkness feel a little less oppressive.

And now I was wide awake.

I snapped on my TV but left it on mute. Company without sound. My phone charged on the nightstand. Usually, I muted that too but tonight I fell asleep before I could. It buzzed softly, inviting my trembling fingers.

I scrolled through social media feeds that blurred into a montage of late-night headlines. Presidential blunders. Music drops and medical discoveries. And then there was Holly. Always Holly, it seemed and now with her new boy toy, Mitch. His face popped up in a tagged photo with her. Sun-drenched, grinning, arms slung around each other like they belonged in some cursed billboard for perfect people.

I hovered over the "block" button for the hundredth time, thumb twitching. But no. Blocking him felt too final. Too dramatic. Too much like admitting I cared enough to need that kind of boundary. So instead, I let myself doom scroll and stew.

News apps spewed updates on the Damian Cross murder. Every twist and turn speculating wildly about both Marradine's involvement and Holly's connections. And now by extension, Mitch's.

I placed my phone back on the nightstand and lay back on my freshly fluffed pillow. The lavender smelled nice, but it also reminded me of the spice of Mitch's cologne. Yeah, I missed him. Like, a lot. It always seemed worse at night, like a fever that slipped over you when your body was run down. If I gave in to it, and on some nights I did more than others, missing Mitch would morph into something more intense...

A portal back to that dim, claustrophobic room...Racer's voice, a hiss like a snake and his stone-cold sharp touch that paralyzed me. I remembered the taste of cheap whiskey, the smell of bitter smoke and stale sex, and the weight of him on top of me. It was all so...heavy. Vivid. It was crazy because when it was happening, and even in recovery at the Dunes, I didn't remember anything at all about it. But now, it haunted me everywhere.

I jerked upright, pulse pounding like a frantic drum. I pressed my palms over my burning eyes. "Fuck you," I muttered with a bitter chuckle that even to my ears sounded deranged. "Pull it together, Nat. You're a distance swimmer. You can beat this."

My own humor amused me, so I laughed. But it wasn't funny. I knew that. Every suppressed memory, every tear I'd refused to shed, pressed down on me. The mounting pressure of academic deadlines, the weight of failing grades, relationships I was incapable of navigating. All of it conspired to remind me that I was spiraling, even as I struggled to hold my life together.

I reached over and picked up my phone from the nightstand. I opened Mitch's contact and poised my thumb over the keyboard to compose a message. But what would I say? Nothing he wanted to hear. Hell, he was probably cock deep in that Holly chick right now and I was a distant memory.

It was almost 5 a.m. now. Pink hues of dawn slipped between the slats of the blinds, and I felt accomplished that I'd won my standoff with the night. But what was my prize? Exhaustion? Keeping all I held close a secret?

This was all running through my mind as I slowly fell back to sleep.

*****'

The next day Staci and I headed down to the gallery for a meeting with one of Lance's artist friends who wanted to commission a painting for the Madsen foundation. I still depended on Staci, Lance, and their constituents to point me on the right path of shrewd business decisions. They knew the industry after all. I just had the good intentions.

I sat shotgun in Staci's Wrangler, soaking up the morning sun and enjoying the wind pushing through my hair. Staci cranked up her favorite alternative rock radio station, so on brand for the "emo diva" vibe she gave off.

"You're not gonna get into trouble blowing off your classes, are you?" Staci teased, glancing over at me with a mix of amusement and concern. "This was the only time he could meet."

"It's no problem. It's just the first week. I'll catch up," I replied, trying to sound nonchalant.

Staci shook her head, smirking. "This guy has a lot of contacts. I wouldn't mind doing his PR work. You know how one client can lead to another."

"Yeah, I guess."

"Having more artists at the gallery thing is great for Lance.

He gets his name out there while he designs his own stuff. You should see the earrings he's making me."

I gave Staci a once-over. I suppose it helped to have someone like Lance who understood both addiction and recovery in her corner. He adored her. And no one could say she didn't appreciate him. So happy and confident, literally in the driver's seat with her right hand draped over the gear shift and her left casually holding the wheel. She wore black pants and a black and white blouse with her long red hair neatly pulled back in a half bun. I, on the other hand, sported a pair of jeans and a black tank top I was pretty sure I washed a few days ago before finding its place draped over my headboard. My hair was up and my only accessories were my aviators. More to hide the bags under my eyes than block the sun.

"Lance had a few other clients today so it's just the two of us meeting this guy." She smiled with pride. "Look at the two of us doing things on our own."

"Look at us," I repeated, trying to match her enthusiasm.

We stopped at a red light and Staci eyed me with a raised brow. "Lance says this guy we're meeting is representing some rich dead guy's estate and has a few pricey pieces he's willing to donate to both the art gallery and your foundation."

I bitterly considered the irony of all the people in this do-gooder scenario who had to die just to raise a few bucks to fund attempts to keep others alive. "I wonder who the rich dead guy was."

"I think I might know."

I lifted my shades to the top of my head and turned down the radio. I had a feeling I knew the answer too. "Who?"

"Damian Cross is rumored to have had a pretty big art collection."

We parked at the curb in front of the gallery. The glass façade with the modern sculptures framing the heavy wooden doors should have made me excited about the prospect of discussing good deeds. Instead, I felt like I was walking a tightrope. White knuckling a balance of best intentions with a terrible anxiety I sported for reasons I couldn't quite articulate.

"So, you really think my little foundation could attract that kind of high-profile person?" I asked, walking around the front of the Jeep.

"That's the whole point of it, right?" Staci replied. "You're still a high-profile person yourself, remember. People are more inspired to be generous if others will know about it."

We walked through the heavy glass door into the three-story lobby. It smelled like lemon and incense, a strange combo that somehow paired well when I heaved in a deep breath. When I first came here years ago while I was still at the Dunes, I was struck by how cool and sophisticated it all was, with the white marble and the winding open staircase and the fountain in the middle. Now it felt homey to me. Soft light through large windows, stark white walls highlighting bright colors on canvas. There were sculptures and ceramics and even novelty furniture.

In the lobby by the foot of the stairs was a line of offices. Lance's assistant, Rain, an intern from UCLA, emerged to meet us through the open door of one of them with another man in tow. Older, forties maybe, impeccably dressed, short dark salt and pepper hair and a quiet warm confidence that made me nervous. He introduced himself as Keith, or Kyle, or Karl— whatever. All I registered was the smug curl of his lips when he said it. We exchanged pleasantries then gathered around a polished conference table discussing paintings he thought would be the perfect centerpieces for the Art for Annie Auction.

"We appreciate you considering donating to us, Mr. Rollings," Staci said. "You certainly sound like you know your stuff as far as art goes."

"Well, thank you, but I'm only going off what my client has told me. You see, the paintings aren't mine. I'm Damian Cross' attorney, and as such, I'm in charge of settling his estate. These paintings are part of it."

Staci nodded. I felt my stomach twist.

"Damian was an eclectic man who loved creativity no matter the medium. Movies of course, music, and he even had a sizeable art collection. There are a few personal pieces we'd be willing to part with. Brody Inez, Damian Cross' partner, doesn't have much interest in fine art. He's more of a 'put carcass on the wall from your latest hunting excursion' kind of guy." He smiled, like he was sharing some benign celebrity gossip.

I didn't smile back.

"So," he said, glancing between us, "I figured this was a good way to clear the books and help a few worthy causes in the process. Good press for the Cross name, too. His legacy could use a bit of polishing, if we're being honest. That little Marradine brat seems to keep bringing the trouble."

Something about the way he said Marradine's name made my skin crawl. I couldn't tell if it was the casual tone or the glint in his eye, like he was already calculating the headlines.

"I see," I said flatly. "Well...that's very generous."

"I do have one thing to ask. That if we do go through with this agreement, that you keep our dealings confidential. We plan on having a press conference of our own to announce the donation when the time is right."

I shrugged and side-eyed Staci who didn't seem like she cared either. "Sure, of course," she said.

I listened intently as he described his interpretation of the four pieces. I understood not bringing them with him, but it would have been nice if he snapped a few pics on his phone or something to see exactly what he was yammering about. But really, what did I know about art dealing anyway? My only question was, if these paintings were so amazing, why was he so into donating them?

Staci took notes and offered suggestions, their faces alight with enthusiasm. I nodded along, but my mind kept straying. What did this guy have to do with Damian Cross? I studied Keith/Kyle/Karl's fingers and noticed how perfectly manicured they were. I wondered when the last time he washed them was. Who or what he had touched since. It was as if every conversation now, art or otherwise, was tinged with bitter distrust.

The meeting wrapped up with promises of follow-up discussions and a tentative timeline for the project. We stepped back into the lobby and saw him out the door. Staci clapped me on the back and smiled. "See? Business acumen isn't all that bad, Nat. Lance would be proud that we handled it all on our own."

"He doesn't seem shady to you?" I asked.

Staci sighed like she begrudgingly agreed. "Let's not judge. We're do-gooders after all..."

She stopped mid-sentence when she saw Lance's open office door across the lobby. We couldn't hear the voices, but we could see the shadows of the people moving around inside.

"I thought Lance wasn't going to be here," I said.

"That's what he told me." Staci shrugged. "That he was meeting with some couple where the guy commissioned him to make a piece of jewelry for his girlfriend or something."

Nothing could have prepared me for what I saw next. Holly Inez and Mitch coming towards us with Lance. The three were deep in conversation and clearly a good one because they were all smiles, regarding some shiny bangle that hung from Holly's wrist.

"I can't believe what I'm seeing right now," I said, fighting the urge to purge my breakfast all over my Converse high tops.

Staci tugged my pinkie finger. "Come on, let's get out of here."

I wanted to make a quick getaway but somehow my feet wouldn't move. I just stood there staring, hating how God damn gorgeous they were. Holly in her pink and white Hollywood-sheik tracksuit, and him sporting his SoCal beach boy khaki shorts and pale blue button down. They were tanned and all smiles, their matching shiny aviators mercifully hiding their presumably bright eyes.

"Natalie?"

The voice hit me like a punch to the gut. I turned, and there they were, Lance, Mitch, and Holly. We all stood in an awkward semi-circle with the hot morning son radiating through the windows. I used that as an excuse to pull down my own shades.

Lance was the first to step forward, all breezy charm in his plain stylish jeans and vintage Sex Pistols t-shirt. "I thought you ladies would have been long gone by now. Do you all know each other?" Lance asked, solely for Holly's benefit of course, because the rest of us all went way back. "Holly, Mitch, this is Natalie Collins and Staci Blinkin."

Staci took the lead, smiling with professional poise and offering her hand. "Of course, we know Mitch. but Holly it's nice to meet you."

"Oh my God you're Natalie Collins, the swimmer!" Holly lifted the shades to her head and extended her hand to me. Her bright white nails looked like claws. "I'm a huge fan!" she beamed. "I mean everyone is, right? American athlete, so patriotic. I'm not athletic at all so I really admire people who are. And everything you've been through and that stuff with that guy..."

When I was convinced her convoluted thought was

complete to her satisfaction, I took her hand and shook it. "Thank you, that's very nice of you."

"I'm sorry I don't mean to embarrass myself. I just really think you're great."

God, I wanted to hate her. I really did. But all I could do was stand there wishing I'd at least washed my hair and swiped on some lip gloss before this accidental meet-cute from hell. I had to admit she was stunning. The kind of stunning that made a messy bun look like a fashion editorial. Long brown hair, cheekbones for days, jade-green eyes that practically glowed, curves in all the right places. Just like everyone else, I only knew her from the Damian Cross murder coverage...and, fine, from my occasional late-night stalking of Mitch's Instagram. Brody Inez's little sister. Marradine Addison's gal pal. And Mitch's very cozy, very convenient "situationship."

"How do you and Mitch know each other, Natalie?" Holly asked sweetly, her head tilting just so, like a cat pretending not to be sizing up the bird.

Everyone turned to look at me. Why was it up to me to explain whatever-this-was? Mitch didn't react, but I saw the subtle set of his jaw. His sunglasses hid his eyes, but I could tell he was scanning me, reading me, calculating...

"From the Dunes," Mitch cut in, casual, cool. "We both work there."

Right. So, that's how we were playing it.

"Yup. Colleagues." I let the word drag, laced with just enough bite to make him flinch, if he was still capable of flinching. "We're very professional."

"So, how'd the meeting about the foundation go?" Lance asked Staci and me. I could tell by the lilt in his voice he was eager to shift the subject.

"Really well," Staci replied. "It was productive."

"That's good to hear," Mitch said, looking at me. "I know how much the foundation means to you, Natalie."

"You all are such kind people." Holly smiled brightly. "And talented, too. Mitch told me about Lance here and all the wonderful work he's produced. The jewelry he designs is truly beautiful, so we had him make a custom piece for me."

I'm sorry...we?

"Isn't it beautiful?" She held out her right arm and fluttered around a silver charm bracelet of sorts. I pretended to admire it while dying inside. "Yeah, it's really pretty," I managed.

"I know this sounds terrible, but I felt like I needed a little pick-me-up, given all the drama going on in this town lately," she added, voice softening like she was in a soap opera.

"Oh, you mean about being a suspect in the Damian Cross murder?"

Yeah, I said it. Couldn't help it.

I didn't need to see it to feel Staci's laser burning glare. She'd warned me more than once about my mouth. *Think before you speak, Natalie!* The Foundation meant playing nice, managing optics, basically keeping the snark to a minimum. I was working on it. I felt bad Holly found her way into my crosshairs. It wasn't her fault she was perfect.

"Well, I guess I'll show you two out," Lance said, gesturing behind him. "Back way's better. The paparazzi's swarming down the road."

"They always are these days," Holly sighed, looping her arm around Mitch's and kissing his cheek like it was habit. "Luckily, I've got Mitch to help me navigate the chaos."

"Yeah," I locked eyes with Mitch through his mirrored lenses. "He's good like that, isn't he?"

Mitch shifted his weight, and I caught the tiniest twitch at the corner of his mouth like he wanted to say something. But what? The last time I saw him he spewed more than I cared to hear.

Once they disappeared back into the building, I couldn't hold it in any longer. "Staci, did you know Lance was working with Holly and Mitch on that jewelry project?"

Staci's shook her head slowly. "No, Nat. I had no idea."

I gulped. "Do you think they're..."

"It certainly looks that way," she said. "I'm so sorry."

I turned away before she could see the reaction I couldn't hide. The ache. The regret. The stupid hope I thought I'd gotten over it all. "Yeah," I said. "I'm sorry, too."

SIX

Re: The Hearing
Dear Mrs. Harriman
January 15, 2:07 am

Thank you again for the reminder about the hearing that's approaching. I composed an email to you, but for whatever reason I noticed it was still sitting in my draft box. It's just as well because more has happened between December 28th at 12:37 am and today and I just thought I would keep you posted as to why I simply cannot make it to Buffalo.

Between work and school, I'm finding myself much busier than I anticipated. Working on my charity foundation is really more than I thought it would be. Meeting with donors and overseeing fundraisers. I also volunteer at the Dunes of course with people who, unlike myself, are still struggling with addiction. I can't just leave all my responsibilities. That would be selfish and selfish is something I was accused of being when I was in the throes of addiction.

I'm sure that it's of popular opinion that appearing at

"

*this hearing would provide me with some closure to all
that's happened to me. The way I see it, I'd just be choosing
to ignore one fire to address one that's long been put out.*

*I assure you I am not trying to avoid it. I am well aware
of how important the hearing is. My mother has been
sending all the updates via Buffalo news, and believe me,
she isn't one to correspond with me unless she has to. Again,
please offer my support to all...*

———

TILLIE'S OFFICE smelled like eucalyptus and the cherry hand sanitizer she kept in a giant bottle on her desk in between her picture of her cat, Louis, and a bowl of fidgets for anxious patients. Funny, this was the one place where I always felt calm. Warm light gathered from high windows; bohemian tapestries hung from soft grey walls. Books with titles like "Emotional Tours in The South of France," and "Be Your Own Sherpa," lined the shelves. Tillie was a homebody herself but loved to read about others' adventures.

I sat on the edge of her puffy grey couch; my hands folded over a red and yellow throw pillow on my lap. Tillie was across from me, notebook on her lap, pen silent. Waiting. This was the part I hated. The entry point. A fresh look at my psyche. It felt kind of like squishing a bug under a book. Who knew what mess you were going to find when you took a peek.

Tillie looked at me with her sweet brown eyes and that little frowny pout of hers. Empathy was her superpower but of course in my fucked-up mind, I saw it as a manipulation. A way to disarm me before stabbing me in the heart. But this was Tillie and that's what she was here to do, rewire my brain so it didn't exist in constant misfire.

"I had another one," I said finally. My voice sounded thin,

like it didn't want to carry across the room. "You know, a bad night."

"A panic attack?"

I chuckled and shook my head. Why label anything? Besides it sounded inaccurate. Like a secret army coordinated some offensive right there in my dark bedroom. "No," I scoffed. "I just kind of freaked out a bit the other night with Eero at the pier. I had a hard time sleeping after."

"Just that night?"

I blew out a breath and studied my hands. "A lot of nights I guess."

She nodded, like she'd known it before I said it. "Do you want to tell me about it?"

I looked past her at the little cactus plant in a planter on the windowsill. I studied the little needles that protruded from its spine. "Same kind of thing as before. Me at Racer's trailer, although it could have been anywhere, I suppose. He was there and he was on me...and my body just...stopped moving.

Tillie nodded. "That sounds terrifying."

"It is...was," I agreed but tried to shore up my compromised wall. "But it's getting better. I'm learning how to get through it."

There was a silence. Not a judgmental one. Just the kind that feels like it's making room for the rest of the truth. Tillie knew it was bullshit. I knew it was bullshit. It was a game of who would call out who first. My right hand pushed up my sleeve on the left. I rubbed my finger pads over the back of my wrist.

"You haven't been at swim practice in over a month," she finally said, shifting slightly in her chair. "How come?"

"How did you know that?"

"I saw coach Mathews the other day when I stopped by campus for a meeting with a colleague of mine. He said he was sorry about your academic probation and wanted me to make sure you got your grades up. You've been removed from the swim team."

I blinked, trying not to flinch at that one. "Temporary suspension," I said automatically.

Tillie tilted her head. "That's not what they called it."

I didn't answer. My throat was tight. Too tight.

"Look, I know I'm still your counselor but after all this time and all we've been through, you know on some level we're friends."

"Of course we're friends. I'm only in therapy because it's with you. You think I would talk about this deep shit with anyone else?"

"Natalie," she asked gently, "are you hiding something?"

My jaw clenched. I didn't mean it to. But I could feel it, the instinct to shut down and lock the doors. The thing Racer taught me to do all too well. "I don't know," I managed.

Tillie leaned forward. "Listen Natalie, you've done a good job dealing with the immediate stuff. Getting clean, school, swimming. But sometimes people go through the physical motions of being okay but don't deal with the mental ones."

"I know that. That's why I'm here."

"But are you really?"

Good question. In fact, I'd gotten pretty good at not really being anywhere these days. Milling around my own mind terrified me, and it wasn't like I wanted to bring others along for a scenic tour. But I didn't mind her practical knowledge and her help deciphering a real-life dilemma. "You know Eero, right? The guy from the swim team?"

"Sure. You told me a few months back you started to see each other."

"I want it to work with him," I told her. "He's really easy to be with, you know? It's like, he's so concerned with his own good time that he couldn't care less about what's going on with me. And I know most girls would feel ignored or not prioritized. But for me, I don't want to be his center of attention."

She gave a small nod but didn't interrupt.

"He lets me go along for the ride," I said, trying to make it clear in my head. "He wants to show me a good time and I let him. That's all."

Tillie rolled her pencil between her fingers and eyed me over the rim of her glasses. "Let me ask you this. Do you want to be with Eero because you like him? Or do you want to be with him because you want to prove you're capable of being with someone."

"I don't know," I said honestly. "But lately I've been second-guessing everything. Not just him. Men in general. Like...maybe I don't even know how to trust any of them anymore. Or I forgot how."

"That sounds like a lonely way to live," she said.

"It is," I admitted, voice small. "But it's better than the alternative."

"What's that exactly?"

I closed my eyes and braced myself. "It's like feeling I'm back in Racer's trailer. On my back in his bed, watching his friends come through the door...knowing exactly what's coming next and not being able to do a damn thing about it so I just let it happen over and over..."

I hadn't meant to say all that, but there it was.

I looked down at the back of my wrist. Rubbed raw again to the point that little pricks of blood bloomed on the surface. I pulled my sleeves down and sat on my hands.

"You're not back in that trailer," she said softly. "But I understand why it feels that way. You were trained to expect betrayal."

That sounded dramatic, but unfortunately accurate.

"It's okay to want connection," she said. "And it's okay to be unsure about how to do that right now. You're still healing, Natalie, and you don't have to perform being okay just to keep someone. Do you think there's a part of you that wants to really let Eero in?"

I let the silence fall again. This time, it didn't feel as heavy. It felt like a pause between breaths. "I don't know," I muttered.

"Not knowing and not knowing how, are two different things," she pointed out. "First though, you have to tend to the wound. You've had a lot of people in your life hurt and abuse you, so now every connection feels like a risk."

"When I left the Dunes, I thought it'd be a fresh start," I said. "New place. New people. New existence beyond Annie's death and all that Olympic meltdown bullshit." My voice caught. "She was the only person who ever *saw* me. And now she's gone."

"But there are still people who are here who love you and who might love you if you gave them a chance."

"But that's too risky," I said. I leaned forward, elbows on my knees, the words finally catching up to the thoughts I'd been chasing for days. "If I stay in control of my feelings, I won't lose control of them. If I don't need anyone, no one can take anything from me. And if I don't feel—" I swallowed, "—then no one can touch me like he did."

The air thickened. It was like I'd spoken something into existence that made the whole room shift. I fanned myself and tugged at the collar of my T-shirt, suddenly hot and claustrophobic.

"What about Mitch?"

My heart kicked against my ribs. "What about him?"

"Did you feel safe with him?"

"Like, I know Mitch isn't going to rape me. Or let his friends do it." I met Tillie's eyes, blinking hard against the sting gathering in mine.

"And what about Eero?" she asked.

"I guess he's a good guy," I said slowly. "Maybe I should give him the benefit of the doubt."

Tillie closed her notebook and folded her hands over it. I could tell by the shift in her expression and the glance she gave the clock, that our session was over. Therapist and headcase: dismissed. She was just Tillie again. My friend. The version of her I loved best, even if the pushy version sometimes got more shit done.

"So, this Paris girl," she said, tilting her head with a half-smile. "Are you planning to say anything? To her or Eero?"

I stood and slung my backpack over my shoulder. "Not sure. I might need to do a little investigating first."

"Good luck," she said, rising too. "But don't let it consume you. People make their choices. You can't control that."

And that right there was the real problem.

Because no part of me believed I shouldn't at least try.

———

That evening, I hit the University field house for a workout with Janessa. Somehow, I was still passing for functional. No one asked questions about swim practice or classes as long as I kept moving fast enough to dodge them. My swipe card still worked, which felt like the universe's way of enabling my denial. Eventually, all the lies might catch up to me. But until then? Fake it, lie about it, pretend you're thriving. Same difference.

I loved the gym. The hum of the machines, the rhythmic pounding of feet on treadmills, and the occasional clang of weights hitting the racks. The smells were great, too. Bleach mixed with BO and rubber. So inspiring. Janessa and I were mid-set at the squat rack, the burn in my quads a welcomed distraction from everything else knocking around my brain.

"Three more," Janessa said, spotting me.

I gritted my teeth, exhaling sharply as I pushed through the last reps. As soon as I racked the bar, I shook out my legs and grabbed my water bottle from the floor.

"Not bad, Collins." Janessa smirked. "You may not have been in the pool much lately, but you're definitely getting stronger."

"Or just angry," I muttered, taking a long drink.

Janessa was about to respond when a shrill laugh cut through the noise.

We both turned. Paris. She stood by the leg press chatting it up with a football player resting between reps. Her sleek blonde hair was pulled into a high ponytail, and even in a plain black sports bra and leggings, she looked like a fashion model. The opposite of me in a baggy grey tee, old biking shorts, sweat-streaked face.

"Oh look, just who we wanted to see," I said, nodding toward the two now flexing for each other, literally and figurately.

Janessa laughed. "She gets around that's for sure. Shit, looks like she's coming over here."

She was. With a strange, crooked smile on her face like she was conjuring up some kind of agenda. I wiped my face with a towel and sighed. "The machine's all yours," I said, when she stopped in front of me.

"That's not what I came over here for," she cut me off. "I actually would like to apologize."

Janessa and I exchanged a look.

"For what?" Janessa asked, voice all sweet venom. "You got something you wanna confess?"

Paris let out a breath like she had to push the words through her teeth. "Yeah...so. It has come to my attention that maybe there were times that I was a bitch at practice. And probably, not just at practice."

"Probably?" Janessa muttered, not bothering to keep it quiet.

Paris ignored her and looked straight at me. "Coach Mathews kept me after yesterday. Said you were taking time away to 'reset your priorities.' He gave me the vibe that you wouldn't have left had I been a better teammate." She let out a dramatic, soap actress breath. "So here I am. Believe me, I wouldn't be doing this if it wasn't required."

I knew it. Even her apologies came with disclaimers. There was no part of me where someone like her would have an effect on my swimming performance. In the pool, my psyche was rock solid. Janessa folded her arms. "So, what is this? Your peace offering?"

Paris gave a shrug, half-effort. "Call it a ceasefire. I've got enough on my plate without petty drama. I figure you'll be back eventually. Might as well keep things civil."

I raised an eyebrow. "That it?"

She tilted her head, eyes cool. Like she had something to say but not sure she should. "Also, maybe keep an eye on your boy."

I laughed. "Excuse me, my boy?"

She smiled, and it didn't reach her eyes. "Just saying, sometimes people pretend they're fine when they're not. Doesn't hurt to check in. Before someone else does."

That hit square between the ribs. She tossed her towel over her shoulder and walked off like she hadn't just lobbed a grenade into my already-frazzled existence.

Janessa let out a low whistle. "Well. That was loaded."

"Extremely."

"You think she's up to something?"

I shrugged, still watching the direction Paris had gone. "Always."

We grabbed our stuff and started toward the weight benches. But as we passed the trainer's office, movement caught my eye.

Eero.

He was leaving, duffel bag slung over his good shoulder, face unreadable. Trainer Martinez stood in the doorway, arms crossed, speaking to him in clipped, low tones. He wasn't arguing, but his jaw was tight, like he was biting back whatever he really wanted to say.

As he turned toward the locker rooms, I caught the slight hitch in his step. The way he adjusted his arm with careful precision, like it was painful to move.

Janessa stilled beside me. "Thought he had class right now."

"He told me he did." We watched him head down the hall without turning back. Janessa frowned. "That doesn't look like someone casually stopping by. That's for sure someone getting chewed out."

"Or covering something up," I murmured.

She glanced at me. "You okay?"

I wasn't sure how to answer that.

SEVEN

"HOLLY INEZ BROUGHT in for questioning! Well, it's about freaking time!" Cassidy practically launched herself off the booth bench, holding her Shirley Temple aloft like she was toasting a revolution. The maraschino cherries bobbed precariously close to the rim. There had to be at least six crammed into the glass, which must have been some kind of health risk if you ask me.

One of our traditions was grabbing dinner at The Barn whenever Ari was back in town. The place was a hybrid sports bar and family restaurant where the burgers were the size of your face, and the fries came in metal buckets. I came for the two-dollar root beer floats. We'd play darts, shoot pool. Gossip. Clearly that was Cassidy's chosen evening activity.

"Hey, Cass," Ari said calmly, patting the vinyl placemat in front of Cassidy like she was trying to coax a kitten out of a tree. "How about you and your TV commentary come down to earth for a minute and join us. We ordered you a grilled cheese."

She was careful not to touch Cassidy's remote. Everyone at this table knew better than to lay a finger on it unless they wanted a lecture, a slap, or both.

"I *knew* that girl had something to do with it," Cassidy said in a much more reasonable indoor voice. "And if she didn't do anything dirty, her brother definitely has."

"Really? Because that's a turn of events I didn't see coming." Staci shook the ketchup bottle over her mountain of curly fries. "Natalie, did Marradine tell you this might be happening?"

I gave her a flat *are-you-serious* look.

"You know what I mean," she said, correcting herself.

The truth was, Marradine hadn't said a word to anyone since she arrived at the Dunes over a month ago. She refused a roommate. She ate alone. She faced the wall when a therapist tried to speak to her. The only person she'd even attempted to communicate with was me and I still had no idea why.

"Do you think she just relates to you somehow?" Ari asked, sipping her soda. "You're both kind of public figures. Maybe she feels like you'd get it. Like, you wouldn't judge her."

"But that's the thing," I said, scooping up a chunk of vanilla ice cream. "She hasn't said *anything* to *anyone*. There's nothing to judge. Tillie says there's precedent for trauma survivors going completely silent. Like their brains are literally too scared to speak."

Staci shook her head. "I'm sorry, I just can't relate to that."

"Not everyone processes things by talking nonstop," Cassidy muttered, dragging a fry through her ketchup. "And who knows what she could be processing."

Lance leaned forward. "The police released the guest list from the party. Pretty much all of Hollywood was there that night—except for Brody Inez. He supposedly reported back to some military base in the Middle East."

"*Allegedly*," Cassidy said.

"What does that even mean?" Ari asked. "How do you fake being deployed?"

Lance shrugged. "Reports say he wasn't actually deployed.

He was supposed to be back filming American Hero Challenge a few days later but hasn't been seen since. Kinda suspicious, right? Like he knew something was about to go down and didn't want to be around for the fallout?"

"And then conveniently ends up being the one to inherit all his dead business partner's assets," Staci added, popping an onion ring from Lance's plate in her mouth.

Ari raised an eyebrow. "I wonder what Mitch knows about all this. I mean, Holly must've confided in him more than just pillow talk."

"Well, that's up to the rest of you to find out," I said coolly. "His girlfriend and her police record don't concern me."

"I invited him, by the way," Ari said casually, grabbing extra napkins from the holder.

Ari had been out of town for work so much over the past year and was still in the dark about a lot of the Mitch stuff. I couldn't blame her for inviting him, and it took too much energy to do so anyway. "Cool," I mumbled.

"Thought it'd be nice to see all my friends at once. And hey, bonus that Holly's not glued to his side tonight. He said she went to San Diego to be with her parents for a bit."

Cassidy laughed. "On TV they don't let suspects leave town. I guess the rules are different in the real world."

The bell above the front door jingled.

In stepped Mitch, looking gorgeously casual in his faded jeans and white tee. He held the door open for an older couple leaving with doggy bags. They thanked him and he smiled. The wide sincere dimpled one. Ever the gentleman. So damn selfless.

"Hey," he said as he reached the table.

Everyone greeted him warmly. Ari jumped up and slung her arms around him. "It's so good to see you!" she said, patting his back with both hands. "You look great."

The only empty seat at the round table was, of course, right next to me. He hesitated for a moment, barely perceptible, before walking around slowly and pulling out the chair. He didn't look at me when he sat, but his presence next to me hit like a wave. Clean soap, sun-warmed denim, and the faintest trace of cologne I thought I bought him for Christmas a few years back.

"Hey." The word caught on the way out. Barely a whisper.

For a few seconds, it was just us in a vacuum. Like the others had faded into white noise. I stared at the condensation running down the side of my root beer float glass. I could feel his shoulder, just inches from mine, and the nearness made my heart stutter in a way I didn't want to admit.

Ari, never one for subtlety, dove right in. "So, Mitch, what's the deal with your gal Holly Inez? Think she did it?"

Staci groaned. "Ari, he just sat down."

"What?" Ari playfully held up her hands in feigned innocence. "I'm on borrowed time here. I fly out in the morning. Might as well fast-track the pleasantries, right?" Ari handed Mitch a menu. "Have something to eat. Catch us up."

He chuckled, but it was hollow. He picked up a leftover chip from the plate on the center of the table, turned it between his fingers, then put it back down.

Ari reached over and patted his hand. "I'm sorry. And I'm half-kidding anyway. You've got that loyal-boyfriend energy. I didn't expect you to throw her under the bus just for gossip."

Mitch scratched his temple and gave a quick glance, almost too quickly, in my direction. "No," he said. "I'd never do that."

Cassidy sighed dramatically. "Oh, well. Worth a shot."

My stomach turned. The vanilla ice cream I'd been enjoying now churned like sour milk. I nudged my half-eaten burger aside.

Shit. It was happening again.

Don't do this here, Natalie!

Suddenly, every sound—the clink of glasses, the crack of pool balls, the bass from the stereo—scraped across my nerves. Mitch's shoulder brushed mine, and I hated how sharply I felt it. Hated that I missed him. That he was inches away but felt a lifetime gone. I yanked up my sleeve and gripped my wrist, my fingers finding the familiar jagged scab...

Pull yourself together, you wimp!

"Yo, Natalie?" Staci pointed to the burger in front of me I didn't even notice was served. "You okay? You said you were starving."

Every eye at the table was on me. A silent scrutiny, it seemed. I stood up, letting the chair scrape loudly over the tile floor. "I'm going to the bathroom."

Without waiting for a response, I headed to the back of the restaurant. My legs were weak, and my feet tingled. My vision started to narrow. I pulled at the collar of my already baggy tee shirt. It felt like I was being strangled or suffocated or maybe having a heart attack the way my chest ached. I made it past the pool table, the dartboard, the music speakers that were so damn loud it somehow hurt my eyes. Finally, I threw open the bathroom door. Just a toilet, a sink and a mirror. Perfect. Smelly but safe.

I leaned over the sink and splashed cold water on my face. My reflection stared back at me through the grey haze of a dirty mirror, and I weirdly appreciated the distortion. I didn't want to see myself this way. Unhinged. Unraveling. Scared...

You brought this on yourself, Natalie. This is all your fault!

And then it hit me, like I'd poked the bear of my own mind. A memory, uninvited and vicious.

Racer's hand locking around my wrists. The stench of his rancid breath. The way the door clicked shut behind me in his trailer, sealing the air off like a tomb...

I forced myself to breathe. One hand on the wall, the other gripping the sink.

You are not there. You are not there. You are not there.

I repeated it like a mantra until the shaking stopped. The cool tile pressed against my back and the fluorescent lights buzzed above. I was exhausted and disoriented. How long had I been in the bathroom? Two minutes? Ten? It could've been an hour for all I knew.

Finally, I forced a breath into my lungs, washed my still-shaky hands, and opened the door.

And, of course, ran straight into Mitch.

I flinched so hard I nearly stumbled backward, but his hand shot out like a reflex and gripped my elbow. I couldn't look him in the eye, so I stared at the center crease of his muscled chest.

"Natalie?" His voice was soft but carried that quiet urgency. "What happened? Are you okay?"

"I'm fine," I said quickly, my throat raw. "I'm fine."

He didn't let go. "You're shaking."

"I said I'm fine."

His hand hovered near my face now, fingertips brushing the air just under my chin like he wanted to make me meet his eyes. But I jerked away before he could.

"Come on, Nat. You won't even look at me now?"

God, that voice. Soft, deep, syrupy smooth. It curled around the edges of my control. Tears welled and I sealed my eyes shut against them. "Will you just leave me alone? Please."

"I'm just asking if you're okay. You looked freaked out when you left the table..."

"That's your thing, isn't it?" I said, my voice rising with the sting of old wounds. "Damsels in distress? Girls you can save? Go back to Holly," I added, bitter. "She seems like she could use a hero right about now."

I finally forced myself to look up at him. God, he always

knew when to shut up and let me twist in my own anger. He didn't yell, didn't defend her, didn't even flinch. Just nodded once, his lips tight.

"Okay," he said quietly. He reached into his pocket and held something out to me.

My phone.

When I didn't take it right away, he placed it in my hand himself. "You left this at the table," he said. "The Dunes called a bunch of times. You might want to call back. Could be about Marradine. You and I both know they wouldn't reach out unless it was urgent."

He didn't wait for me to reply. Instead, he gave me one of those wrinkled brow, concerned once-overs, a slight tug of my fingers I interpreted as a "I delivered my message, so my job is done here" gesture, and headed back to the table.

For a second, I just stood there, willing my heartbeat into a normal cadence. From my vantage point, I could see him say his goodbyes to everyone. He'd probably made some lame excuse. Like he had work or was tired and the gang would claim to understand, but they would all know he was leaving because of me. I made things hard. Awkward and dramatic. I was the problem. Someone to be handled. Suddenly my phone vibrated in my hand. This time a text. From Tillie. I opened it.

Tillie: Call me ASAP! Marradine wants to talk to you!

I sighed. Maybe all the drama that surrounded me wasn't always just my fault.

I headed back to the table and said my own goodbyes.

———

Nighttime at the Dunes had a different energy. Not exactly lonely, but quieter. Still. During the day, distractions came in waves in group sessions, structured activities, staff check-ins. At night, without all that noise, the silence allowed your thoughts to infect you. Night was like a painfully patient instigator who held a mirror to your mind's eye and waited for you to flinch.

Between what happened to me at the restaurant and not sleeping well the night before, by the time I arrived I was running on caffeine and nerves. Somehow, Tillie always knew when I was stretched too thin. She met me at the front with a paper cup of chamomile tea already in hand.

"I needed this," I muttered, letting the steam sting my face before taking a sip. I leaned against the conference room door. "So, what's this about, you think?"

Tillie shrugged. "Not sure. A couple nurses said Marradine was in the dayroom earlier, watching the news coverage about Holly Inez. Something about her being tied to the Damian Cross investigation." She glanced at me. "Feels like more than a coincidence."

That tracked. But it didn't clear up what exactly I was supposed to do. Technically, I was just a volunteer here. A glorified helper. Hell, I still had my own messes to clean up. Marradine saw me as a friend, sure. I just hoped she didn't see me as a role model. I wasn't that. Not even close.

"What am I supposed to do in there?" I asked. "How do I act?"

"Just be an ear," Tillie said simply. "You're good at that." With a comforting pat on the back, she sent me down the hall toward the visitor's office.

The room was warm and familiar, with its overstuffed couch, ergonomic recliners, a few hardy houseplants, and the faint scent of sandalwood lingering in the air. Soft lighting made it feel more like a cozy den than a clinic room.

Marradine, as always, sat upright in the desk chair rather than on the couch. We had this routine where I would sit across from her, and we'd mime and pass notes between us like a salesman and customer haggling the sale of a used car. It was part of our unspoken rhythm. It worked for us, or at least it had so far.

She wore a white Dunes sweatshirt and standard issue white pants, her auburn hair spilling down in loose waves like curtain ties. She gave me a small smile and a nod that I took as a quiet thank-you.

"I brought the good stuff," I said, placing a cup of mocha latte Tillie made to give to her. "Sorry I took longer than I meant to. It took a minute for them to get a hold of me."

Her eyes flicked to the drink, then back to the sketchpad between us. She picked up her pencil; hesitated. Erased something. Started again. Erased it once more.

On the third try, she scribbled something quickly, tore out the page, and slid it across the desk toward me.

You see the news about Holly Inez?

I blinked. Not what I expected. I'd thought we'd ease in, do the usual routine of scribbled sarcasm and one-word answers before circling anything real.

"Yeah," I said, leaning back slightly. "Called in for questioning today. I heard she's staying with her parents somewhere out of town."

Before I finished speaking, she was already writing again. The second note came faster this time.

She doesn't know anything. Tell the police to leave her alone.

A chill crawled up my spine. "How do you know?"

Her lips pressed into a tight line. Her pencil moved furiously.

Because I saw her leave with her boyfriend that night. She wasn't there when he was murdered.

I froze.

There was a sharp twist in my gut. I wasn't sure what scared me more, the fact that she said it so plainly, or how natural my next question felt.

"Marradine...were you with Damian that night?"

She didn't hesitate this time. She already had the next note ready.

Holly and Damian are good people. She had nothing to do with what happened to Damian.

I swallowed hard, trying to keep my hands steady.

"You were in the room?"

Her pencil hovered, then moved slower now, like every word cost her something. She tore out the paper and slid it over.

I think so...

She didn't finish the sentence. But I didn't need her to.

I steadied my breath. "Did you kill Damian, Marradine?"

Her head snapped up. She shook it violently and immediately scribbled:

NO! DAMIAN IS A GOOD MAN!

The pencil marks were hard, angry slashes. My hands tightened in my lap. I wasn't a cop, or a therapist. I wasn't qualified for this. But I also knew what it felt like to carry something heavy and have no one you trusted to set it down with.

I leaned forward. "Marradine, was Damian...doing things to you?"

She flailed, head shaking wildly. Her hand snatched the pencil and tore through the page.

No! Damian is not a creep! It's not safe to say any more! Holly knows nothing! She was my friend!

"Why didn't you say this before?" I asked quietly.

This time, she looked right at me. Her eyes were glassy but clear and focused. She began to write slowly.

Because no one listens. People think I'm some crazy, spoiled, Hollywood brat. Maybe I am. But

that doesn't mean I'm not a person. There are things about me that no one knows. But please hear me now. If I remembered more, I'd say more. I'm only telling you what I *know*. Everything else will have to wait.

"Everything else?" I asked. "What does that mean?"

Not until I know for sure.

"Okay, okay," I said, holding up my hands, trying to calm the spike in her breathing. "But if you *do* know something, or if someone's hurting you, you have to let people in. You can't keep carrying that alone."

Her eyes flashed. She scribbled furiously, then shoved the paper toward me.

You're one to talk. How's that guy in Buffalo?

I flinched. Cheap shot. But she wasn't wrong. I was sort of a hypocrite. I didn't respond right away. Just took a breath and steadied myself. "Is there anything else you want me to know?"

Her pencil paused again, slower now.

No. And I won't say more until it's safe. You're the only one I trust. You're not going to tell anyone I said this, right?

I shook my head. "Of course not. Besides, I couldn't even if I wanted to. You told me in confidence. That means something."

She nodded slowly like she understood. Or maybe just that she wanted to. When she shut her notebook and turned back toward the window, I knew our time was up.

I stood and headed toward the door. "I'm gonna look into this, Marradine," I said. "We'll stick together on this. I've got your back."

She didn't respond. Just kept her eyes on the glass, like something was waiting out there she couldn't quite see.

EIGHT

THAT NIGHT the ocean outside my bedroom was especially rough. Just wave after wave pulling at the shore like it was trying to reach me. I'd tried everything to sleep. All my rituals, herbal tea, white noise, even reading the most boring European History textbook from a course I failed out of. Nothing worked.

I lay in bed, staring up at the ceiling fan. My legs were tangled in the sheets, my chest tight. The conversation with Marradine kept replaying in my head like a bad loop. Her voice, ink on paper, still echoed louder than most people's spoken words.

My phone buzzed on the nightstand. The screen lit up, and I blinked against the harsh blue glow.

Mitch: You up?

I stared at the screen for a long second. Of course I was up. I was practically vibrating with tension, adrenaline, confusion, take your pick. What the hell was he texting me for? I thought I'd blocked him and then I remembered I "forgot" to.

My thumbs hovered over the keys. If it weren't for my meeting with Marradine, I might have left him on read. At least I would have liked to think I would have. But what she confided in me about gave me a reason to respond. So, I did. I sat up and took a deep breath.

Me: Yeah. Why?

Mitch: Can we talk? I'm outside.

My heart stumbled into a weird rhythm. I got out of bed, shoved my feet into the nearest pair of flip-flops, grabbed my black hoodie and pulled on sweats over my shorts. The hell with my hair or anything else. He'd seen me worse off.

The house was dark and quiet. Cassidy was asleep in front of the TV in the living room, a nature documentary still playing to an audience of one. The light over the stove was on illuminating the permanent mess the kitchen had been in for the past few days preparing for Cassidy's aunt to arrive. It reminded me that life hadn't been interrupted for anyone, even if I felt mine was in limbo.

I slipped through the sliding glass door and stepped out onto the deck. The beach was silver in the moonlight, the surf glowing like it was lit from underneath. Mitch stood at the edge of the sand, his hands shoved deep in his jean pockets, navy blue windbreaker zipped up, shoulders hunched. His favorite Denver Broncos cap held a shadow over his face.

I walked down the steps slowly, heart thudding in my ears. He didn't move until I was a few feet away, when he turned to face me.

"Hey," he said, barely audible over the waves.

"Hey," I replied, trying to sound aloof.

We stood like that for a second, just the two of us and the ocean and everything we used to be. I hated how much I missed him. How familiar he still felt. How part of me wanted to reach for his hand just to know I still could.

"I shouldn't be here," he said, finally breaking the silence. "But I couldn't sleep. I didn't like how things went between us tonight."

I crossed my arms, trying to block the cold and the ache in my chest. "So, what is this? Some sort of guilty check-in? Or you didn't get the reaction from me you wanted, so you came here to try again?"

He looked away, out at the water, kind of smiling to himself. He was always so mature like that. Letting me have a tantrum like a parent does a toddler before appeasing them with calm rationale. "No, Natalie. Not at all. I'm just worried about you."

A bitter laugh escaped my throat. "Why? Because you're starting to realize the person you replaced me with might not be as innocent as you thought? Maybe that's why she skipped town like her brother."

"How did you know Holly was out of town?"

"You wouldn't be here if she wasn't."

I stood tall trying to feel confident in the space. Funny how he always seemed to loom large over me with his big football build and broad shoulders. He looked smaller tonight. Less imposing against the vastness of the ocean. When his eyes met mine, I noticed their usual deep blue was dull, darker. Like he was tired or stressed, maybe sad. "Natalie, I never replaced you."

"Sure feels like it," I snapped. "One minute you're here and the next you're posing on red carpets with Holly Inez."

"I didn't go out looking for someone else," he said. "It just... happened."

"Right. Like a car accident."

"It wasn't like that."

I took a step closer, my voice lower now, sharper. "Then what was it like, Mitch? Because from where I'm standing, it looks a hell of a lot like you traded in a broken Natalie for a shinier, more Instagram-friendly version."

His face twisted into something like very focused anger with the way his nostrils flared and his jaw set. "You left me, Natalie!

You were the one who pushed me away! I thought we were happy..."

"You rejected me, Mitch! Understand you were the one steady thing in my life from the moment I left my old fucked up one in Buffalo and you brought me to the Dunes..."

"I didn't reject you!"

"Then what would you call what happened?" I shoved him hard in the chest, but he barely flinched. "You were supposed to look out for me!"

"I did and I have! That's what I was doing that night!" he screamed, louder than I thought he was capable. He must have surprised himself because he blew out a breath to calm himself. "Look, I know there were blurred lines as far as me working at the Dunes and you being a resident. But we NEVER were unethical! It was over a year after you left that I did anything more than hold your hand! You know that!"

"Yeah, you're so ethical all right! To a fault!"

"Natalie..."

"I was swimming and in school and you were working and finishing your PhD. You're a fucking doctor working for the military now for fuck's sake!"

"Exactly and I know a sexual trauma victim when I see one. I wasn't going to take advantage of you."

"Don't call me a victim," I snapped. "I'm no wimp!"

"And I'm not an idiot!" he grabbed my arms and forced my gaze to meet his. "You think the nights I slept beside you I didn't hear you get up and pace the floor? You think I didn't notice those nervous ticks you have now? Like the way you pick at your shirt sleeves and rub your skin raw?"

I jerked myself away and discreetly pulled my sleeves down over my hands. "You have no idea what you're talking about," I mumbled.

"I know exactly what I'm talking about," he said softly. "Because I know you, Natalie."

He again stepped toward me, so close I could feel his heat. My stomach flipped but I couldn't name why. Sick, sad, scared... "I wanted you, Mitch," I said, my eyes fixed out at the water. "I needed you. I fucking threw myself at you..."

"Yeah, you did." He cut me off. "But I didn't want us being together to be about some game you were playing with yourself, or some warped experiment you were staging. Do you know how much it breaks my heart to think about what that guy did to you?"

"All I know is *your* betrayal that night felt worse than what Racer did to me over and over."

Yeah, I said it.

My sucker punch clearly landed. He looked stunned. Truly gutted, but I didn't care. I was tired. I was raw. I'd been holding this in for way too long. I stepped back and threw my hands in the air. "I can't talk about this anymore. There's nothing more to say about it anyway."

Mitch nodded and I saw a glaze in his eyes that reflected the moonlight. He discretely ran his thumb over his cheek. "Look I have another reason for being here. To want to talk to you."

"Okay, shoot."

"Ethical or not, I'm still listed as one of your counselors at the Dunes, so I'm informed when there're additions to your chart."

I hugged myself against the cold. "What do I care about that? I'm not there anymore and what could I possibly hide from you that you don't already know about me?"

"A Mrs. Harriman, a representative from the Niagara County Supreme Court in Buffalo, is trying to get in touch with you. She wants you to come to Buffalo to give a victim impact speech at Racer's sentencing. She says she's tried to contact you for months and you haven't responded."

The light breeze could've knocked me over. My whole body went still, like my nerves short-circuited. My eyes locked on the water, watching the foamy white waves drift toward shore. "I was going to," I said, my voice coming out thinner than I meant. "I planned on it. I just..."

"You planned on responding to the woman or going to Buffalo?" he asked. "The message she left said she's tried every way to get to you. Mail, social media. Her last-ditch effort was calling the Dunes..."

"I don't need to go to any hearing."

He took a step toward me again and I braced myself for his proximity. "Natalie, we talked about this. You can't just shake off sexual assault. Especially in your case when it happened over and over again. This is a whole separate issue than addiction or swimming or Annie."

I winced at the mention of Annie's name. "Please don't play psychiatrist with me right now. Just be Mitch."

He shook his head. "Okay look, I'm so sorry this is what happened between us. This is the opposite of how I wanted this to play out. And Holly...it's not what you think."

"It doesn't matter what I think," I said, as both a statement and a reminder to myself. I looked down at my feet, watching the edge of my flip flop draw a line in the sand. "Look, while you're here I have a question I wanted to ask you."

He raised an eyebrow. "What?"

"What do you know about Damian Cross?" I asked flatly. "And why is your girlfriend suddenly being questioned in his murder?"

Mitch's face went pale. "That call tonight from the Dunes was about Marradine after all, huh? She's talking to you?"

I didn't answer. I wouldn't betray Marradine's trust.

He exhaled, like something heavy had just landed on him. "Holly just tried being a friend to Marradine. Marradine's the new It Girl with a bad reputation. Maybe you can relate?"

I shrugged. "Perhaps."

"Holly is a nice girl who hangs out with her big brother a lot who happens to be Damian Cross' partner. When she saw Marradine was struggling, she tried to be a big sister. That's all."

I scoffed. "That's really all?"

"Yes," he insisted. "She's not some sophisticated calculating liar. She's just a nice, naïve sweet girl who likes to see the good in people."

I laughed at the irony. "The opposite of me, huh? Must be a refreshing change."

He hesitated. A cold wind swept off the water, and I pulled my hoodie tighter around me. We stood in silence for a long moment. The air between us felt like glass, thin and breakable. "Look despite what the press says, Holly's talk with the police was just routine. But I don't want you caught in the middle of it."

I stared at him. "Me?"

"You think I don't still worry about you, Natalie?" He looked at me for a long moment, his eyes suddenly full of regret. "Are you sleeping with that Eero guy?"

I flinched. A question I didn't expect. "So, what if I am?" I blurted, meaning to sound vague with a tinge of vindictiveness. "If it feels good for both of us, why not, right?"

The moonlight caught the side of his face, and I could see the disappointment in his expression. I wasn't someone who looked for payback. Yeah, he'd hurt me but that didn't mean I was out to do the same.

"I should go," I said, turning toward the deck.

"Natalie," he called after me.

I stopped.

"Please think about going to that hearing in Buffalo. I think it would be good for you. And I'm here if you need me. Just come find me."

I chuckled. Like I would seek him out after he pushed me so far away? The ocean was still pulling at the shore. The full moon still glimmered above. Such a romantic setting wasted. "Mitch, did you really think I would just swoon and come back to chase after you?"

"Are you kidding me? Natalie Collins, the fastest swimmer in the world doesn't chase anyone. You think I don't know that by now?"

———

A few days later was the event the beach house crew had been prepping for. It was a full-blown operation. You'd think we were hosting royalty, not Cassidy's aunt, but in a way, Aunt Rose Celeste Judith Fontaine might've been even worse. Royalty waved and smiled. Aunt Rose scowled and judged.

At the beach house, the division of labor was clear: I handled cleaning duty. This wasn't up for debate. It was universally agreed that while I was a disaster in the kitchen, I had a serious gift with a mop (when I was motivated to use one). By the time I was done, the house smelled like lemon cleaner and bergamot candle, a scent combination that practically screamed, *We're trying way too hard, but please notice how clean everything is!* There. I did my part.

Staci, Lance, and Ari had gone full Rachael Ray with the food. They didn't just plan a menu; they storyboarded an experience. The kitchen table looked like it belonged in a lifestyle magazine. Glossy fruit tarts arranged in hypnotic spirals, delicate shortbread dusted with just the right amount of powdered sugar, and miniature cucumber sandwiches that kept collapsing if anyone so much as breathed near them. Ari had carved the scones into uniform triangles, which Lance dubbed "aggressively hospitable." Staci, not to be outdone, had laid out a full tea service with almost religious precision. Bone china cups she found on Marketplace sat beside three varieties of loose-leaf tea. Fancy. We were ready! Let the manipulation begin!

Meanwhile, in the living room, we were trying to prep Cassidy like she was about to sit down for a deposition.

"Just follow our lead," Staci said, straitening the straps on Cassidy's white sundress. "Be polite, nod a lot, and maybe don't talk about the Topanga commune incident. Or your aura."

Cassidy frowned. "But my aura's been very clear lately. I've been watching a lot of Hollywood Medium."

"But still, don't bring it up," Ari cut in. "And definitely no stories about the tarot reading you did for that guy at the gas station."

"He said it was life-changing."

"He also paid you in scratchers," Ari replied.

"And I won two dollars." Cassidy plopped onto the couch and crossed her arms. "So, you basically want me to pretend I'm someone else?"

"No," I said gently, smoothing down the fly aways from Cassidy's blonde ponytail. "We just want her to see the version of you we see. The one who's grounded and brave."

She seemed to soften at that. "You think I'm brave?"

"Definitely," I said. "Like, that took a lot of guts when you tried to smudge the mailman last week?"

Cassidy smiled. "I was clearing his energy."

"Exactly," I replied. "But just for today, leave the energy alone, okay?"

The knock came right at noon, sharp and intentional. Staci put her hand on the doorknob then turned over her shoulder to give us one last once-over. "You guys ready? Remember, agree to everything she says and make sure she knows Cassidy is happy here and is capable of living with us. Best behavior."

We looked at each other, assessing our sundresses and golf shirt preppy ensembles. Despite the random tattoo peeking out from a sleeve here or there, we cleaned up well.

"Wait!" Cassidy snapped. She pulled her remote from somewhere under her dress leveled it at the door and pressed the play button. "Okay, I'm ready."

"Mrs. Fontaine," Staci greeted when she pulled the door open. "Welcome to our home! Come right in!"

Aunt Rose stepped into the beach house like she was entering a country club she didn't entirely approve of. Tailored beige slacks, a white silk blouse tucked in with military precision, a strand of perfect pearls around her neck. Her short ash-blonde bob looked like it hadn't moved since Reagan was in office. Her heels were soft-soled and narrow, the kind you wore to quiet your steps, not take them.

Her eyes flicked from the hanging string lights to the surfboard propped near the fireplace. "This is...charming," she said after a long beat. Her voice was tight and perfectly pitched, like she might faint if she saw a throw pillow out of place. "Very quaint."

Cassidy ran up and hugged her. Rose returned the gesture with polite restraint, patting Cassidy's back like she was allergic to emotion. "You look...well," she said, giving Cassidy a once-over. "Though I must ask, what's all over your skin?"

"It's healing glitter," Cassidy offered cheerfully. "For my aura."

We all shared a quick glance. So close.

Rose made a face when she noticed some sticking to her. She brushed it off with brisk motions. "I see."

We'd all gathered in the living room making small talk over snacks. Lance, Ari, Staci and I stuck to eating only what didn't make a mess, spill or stain. Cassidy, of course, went right for the cherry custard creme puffs. Lance hovered with a napkin ready for emergency cleanup.

"So," Rose began, folding her hands like she was preparing for cross-examination. "You're the group proposing a custodial arrangement."

"It's not as official as that," Staci jumped in. "We're not filing paperwork or anything. But Cassidy's happy here. She's safe, cared for. It feels right."

Rose turned to Staci with a cool smile. "Yes, I'm sure it *feels* many things. But we don't build lives on feelings. We build them on structure. Permanence. Supervision."

Cassidy leaned in then, her voice small but clear. "But I do feel all those things here. That's why I want to stay."

Rose glanced at her, the edges of her mouth tightening slightly. "You've said that before. About the group home. About that commune in Topanga. Although neither one of those places was a great choice. I suppose I should be thankful that crazy vegetable boy is long gone."

"Kevin was a nice boy," Cassidy said quickly. "I'm sorry he's gone but I have my friends here which is just as nice."

Rose studied her niece, then looked at the rest of us. "And who pays the rent here?"

"We do," Staci said. "The gallery's been doing well. And we all chip in."

"And Staci's parents are rich," Cassidy quipped. "They have just as much money as you have."

Staci took a sip of her punch and shrugged. "Well, she's not wrong."

"So, there's no formal guardianship," Rose pressed. "No insurance oversight. No educational plan. No therapy coordination."

"We can work that out." I said. "All of us can pitch in."

Rose's expression was unreadable. "Well, it's very modern of you. A household with no designated structure or supervision."

"I'm not a pet," Cassidy snapped. "I don't need a leash."

"No," Rose said coolly. "But you do need to be protected."

The silence in the room was thick. Ari finally broke it, her voice soft. "So, what do you want, Rose? For her to go back to a group home? Why should anyone live where they don't want to when she can be with people who love her like we do?"

Rose hesitated. I saw something flicker across her face. Concern maybe. Or doubt. But then resignation.

It passed quickly. She reached into her purse and pulled out a pair of silver rhinestone cheaters and a folded piece of legal paper. "I would like to speak with her social worker and get some insight from them on this situation. I already called the Dunes and while I realize she hasn't been there in quite some time, I was given two names." She cleared her throat and eyed the paper. "A Matilda Jefferies—"

"Tillie!" I blurted. "She's great. And she knows all of us well."

"Wonderful, and a Mitchell Winslow. I'm told he's a psychologist who specializes in cases like hers. He didn't work on her case directly at the time, but that pleases me if he could give an objective assessment of how she is now."

Cassidy rolled her eyes. "Can you talk to me like I'm here? I have ears you know and it's not like I put you on mute!"

Ari eyed me from across the table. "We know Dr. Winslow also."

"In passing," I interrupted. "And you're right, he wasn't directly involved with any of our cases so I'm sure he would be very objective."

Rose took a sip of her coffee and dabbed the side of her mouth with her napkin. "If this...arrangement is going to continue, it needs to be legally sound. And it needs account-ability."

"I'm not going anywhere," Cassidy voice wavered. "This is my home. Please Aunt Rose."

Cassidy's lower lip trembled, and her eyes glistened with tears. She was like a little sister to me, and I wouldn't let her go without a fight. "Mrs. Fontaine, I promise she'll be well taken care of. And I'm here most of the time. We're all here for each other."

Rose turned her gaze on me like a microscope focusing in. "You're Natalie Collins, correct? You're the famous swimmer."

"Yes, that's me."

"*Former* swimmer," Cassidy chimed in helpfully, with a mouth full of creme puff. "Natalie got thrown off the swim team after she failed out of college."

The room fell silent.

Cassidy looked around, confused by the sudden drop in energy.

"Cassidy, that's not important right now," I said.

"The envelope from the university that came last week looked super important. I figured you thought so too because you hid it pretty well in your room. Took me a while to find it."

I made a mental note to revisit our discussion on privacy and boundaries and reading other people's mail being a federal offense. "Cass that's not quite what's up for discussion right now..."

"At first I felt really bad for you, but then I realized you'll just have more time to hang around with me." She smiled to herself and crammed the last of her pastry in her mouth.

Staci stepped in, ever the peacekeeper. "Natalie is just reprioritizing. She's busy running a nonprofit, mentoring at the Dunes, and is currently planning a major fundraiser. She's more than capable."

"I'm sure she's *very* committed," Rose said, in the same tone one might use to describe a particularly earnest dog. "But you must understand my concern. Cassidy is fragile. She needs stability."

"I *am* stable," I said before I could stop myself. "We all are. Cassidy needs to be here with us. It's what best for her. I promise you."

Rose didn't argue. She just stood and smoothed her slacks. "I'll be in touch."

And just like that, she was gone.

"So! that went well," Lance declared with a sarcastic clap of his hands when the door closed behind him.

Did it? The best I could figure was that I had some explaining to do.

NINE

LATER THAT NIGHT, Eero took pity on my trainwreck of a day and dragged me out for burgers at The Barn. Eero had been away in Boston for almost a week, so it was nice to catch up with him. He didn't mention any injury to his arm or a confrontation with his trainer and I didn't bring up Damian Cross or my own private drama, so we just existed in this very easy bubble of denial. Truthfully, we hadn't talked much at all since he'd been gone. Anything deeper than what kind of fries to order seemed beyond our emotional wheelhouse.

Even though it was just the two of us, Eero and I slid into our gang's usual corner booth. We were halfway through a second basket of popcorn, and I was nursing a peanut butter milkshake thick enough to bend the straw.

"This is so good," I mumbled, licking the rim. "They should really offer free refills on these."

Eero paused mid-bite of his burger, eyeing me. "That bad, huh?"

"I don't know. It *feels* pretty bad, that's for sure." I laughed, but really I just wanted to cry. "I guess it just feels like every aspect of my life is imploding and I can't control any of it."

"It's too bad your friends had such a strong reaction. I mean, it's your business. You have a right to keep your own secrets. You could have told me though."

"There was nothing to tell. Or at least, nothing worth knowing."

Eero shrugged and took a bite of his burger. I realized that if the roles were reversed, that if *I* were the one finding out my boyfriend had lied to my face about important parts of his life, I'd be angry too. I'd feel like my feelings didn't matter. That's how everyone else reacted. After Aunt Rose left, I endured a full-scale interrogation from the group. Even Cassidy said my silence felt worse than being wrong about who "The Masked Singer" really was.

Another reason why Eero was so appealing. His indifference.

"What would you have said if I told you?" I asked him.

He took a swipe of his mouth with his napkin. "What do you mean? Told me you got booted from the school and all that?"

"Yeah, when you put it that way..."

"For real?"

It felt like he was building up to something. Something he wasn't sure I'd take well. He crumpled his napkin, dropped it on his plate, pushed it aside, and let out a slow breath.

"Here's the thing," he said. "I know I'm a guy, and maybe being from Europe, I see things differently than, like, all these spacey, self-obsessed California types. But I'm wondering if it's time you just...got over it."

I blinked, unsure where this left turn was taking me. "Got over what?"

"All of it," he said, like it was obvious. "I mean, yeah, I know you've had a rough time. The Olympic meltdown, losing your friend, going through that rehab program, and that guy back in your hometown. The one who did all that messed up stuff to you." He shook his head like the summary alone exhausted him.

"Yeah," I said quietly. "It's been really hard."

"But it's over," he insisted. "That guy's in jail, right? It's all behind you now. And honestly, maybe it's a blessing you don't remember much of it."

"I remember enough," I said flatly. "Believe me."

He shrugged. "Well, maybe it's time to forget. And with Annie, she'd want you to move on, too. Life is for the living, right? You're never going to be able to move on unless you move on."

I stared at him, speechless. In one way, he made sense. In another, more *real* way, I wanted to punch him in the face. "So, what exactly do you suggest I do?" I asked.

"Take a break," he said carefully, like he was testing the idea as he said it.

"How?" I let out a short laugh. "I'm barely keeping it together as it is. I need to re-enroll in classes, pull my grades up if I ever want to get back in the pool. There's my mentorship with Marradine, and the auction next month. Lots of stuff."

Eero's expression softened. He reached across the table, his thumb brushing against mine. "You have a way of stacking your chaos, Nat," he said. "But seriously, come away with me. Just for a weekend. Get out from under all this pressure."

I was about to answer when he reached for his right shoulder and made a scrunched-up face when he rubbed it.

"Your arm has been bothering you, hasn't it," I asked.

He blinked, then grinned like I'd asked something silly. "It was a little stiff last week maybe. So what?"

"Paris mentioned it and I saw you with the trainer."

Eero laughed, rolling his eyes. "Paris just likes to rattle your cage, Natalie. Everything's fine."

I nodded, though something about the way he said it didn't quite land right.

"Then again," he continued. "Maybe it's the universe telling the both of us we could use some rest and relaxation. We should go away."

I literally laughed out loud. "Go where?"

"Doesn't matter," he said. "Santa Barbara. Joshua Tree. Anywhere without Wi-Fi or people who know your name. Just make some good memories. Something to outshine all the bad ones. You've been clinging so tightly to everything that's happened. Maybe it's time to let go."

To a normal, mentally-sound person, that would be a hell of a pitch. Some hot guy wants to whisk me away for a weekend of fun and games. To Headcase Me, it sounded like a trap. Saying "yes" to Eero came with a string of expectations that would only escalate if we disappeared together for an overnight.

I looked down at my milkshake, stabbing the last stubborn chunks of ice cream with my straw. "I get what you're saying," I murmured. "I want to have fun."

"Then let's try," he said softly. "Just for one weekend."

The idea floated between us, fragile but intoxicating. And in that moment, I realized how much I craved it. Not just the escape, but the permission to stop holding everything up for a little while.

"Okay," I said finally.

"Great. I'll plan everything," he said, practically buzzing. "You don't have to do a thing. Just be ready when I pick you up."

I laughed despite myself. "Okay, when?"

"This weekend. Friday," he said. "I'll check out some Airbnbs."

As I sat there, sipping the last of my milkshake, I let myself pretend, just for a minute, that all my life's problems could be solved with a weekend in someone else's condo. It wasn't true. But it wasn't like I had any better offers...

———

Dear Marradine
January 21, 3:22 a.m.

Just letting you know, I'm going away this weekend with my boyfriend Eero. Have I told you about him? I can't remember. I've swam with him for a few years, but we've really only been dating for a few months. A part of me is looking forward to going but another, way bigger part wants to hide under my bed until Monday.

Not that it's overly important that you know this, and maybe you already do know it because sex scandals are always high profile... But, before I went to the Dunes I was basically whored out to drug addicts by a man twenty-five years older than me. This was back in Buffalo, after I had that mental breakdown at the Olympic press conference. Anyway, I considered this guy my boyfriend. I was convinced he loved me. That he was someone I could trust.

It's amazing what a human can talk themselves into.

When everything hit the press while I was at the Dunes, I didn't think it would affect my life moving forward very much. I didn't remember much of it anyway since I was so messed up, when a lot of the bad shit happened. But now with a clear head, some of the memories I thought didn't exist have filtered back into my brain. They crop up in weird moments. The worst moments. I'm not sure if I should be embarrassed by it. But mostly, I'm secretly terrified.

I have no idea why I'm telling you all of this, and right now, randomly in this letter. Maybe because I just needed to get it off my chest before I head into this situation with Eero. I also wonder if you could relate...been in a position where people you've trusted have taken advantage of you.

The thing is, sometimes I now wonder, after everything, if I don't even give people the chance to earn my trust in the first place. Maybe I should think about that on my weekend away with Eero.

Best,

Natalie

———

I didn't want to go. And it wasn't like I had a specific list of reasons or one glaring deal-breaker keeping me home. I just Did. Not. Want. To. Go. Bed-rotting, eating junk, and listening to Cassidy scream at Love Island felt like a much better use of my weekend.

The thing was, I did like Eero. He was good to me. And bailing on him now would've been colder than he deserved. So, I spent the morning in a flurry of half-hearted activity. Packing, unpacking, re-packing, washing my hair, moisturizing.

Staci, Ari, Cassidy, and Janessa flitted in and out of my bedroom that looked like Beirut on a bad day. We matched outfits with shoes and considered the need for jewelry. Staci finally perched herself on the bed, matching socks. I ended up on the floor, fishing for their mates in the abyss under my dresser.

Staci sighed, folding a light sweater with the kind of care only people not wearing it ever applied. "Maybe this is what you need. A couple of days away to clear your head and get some perspective."

"I just wish you'd told us what was going on earlier," Ari added gently from where she sat folding tank tops. "The grades, the swim team...the way you've been shutting us out. We could've helped."

"I didn't need help," I said, even though we all knew that wasn't true. "I just got lazy. I let it all snowball."

"You've never been lazy," Staci said. "And you're really okay? You don't think you need more time with Tillie or maybe even..." she paused, "...someone else?"

I stood up to look at her. "You mean Mitch?"

She didn't deny it. "I wish you'd just tell us what happened with him," Staci said. "You know how he feels about you."

"He doesn't feel anything anymore," I muttered, dumping a pile of wrinkled shirts onto the bed. They'd been sitting in a basket for a week. I hadn't even bothered to fold them.

"Are you serious?" Ari asked. "It's obvious to everyone. The way he looks at you. It's like he sees nothing or no one else."

"You're so dramatic," I deflected, brushing her off. "Besides, it doesn't matter. He's with Holly now."

"She's his second choice and you know it," Cassidy chimed in as she entered the room, arms full of sparkly nonsense she insisted I needed. "Mitch just picked the girl who didn't make things hard. You're the one who made him feel something."

I scoffed. "Kind. Sane. She's got things he needs that I'm not."

"She's not you," Ari said simply, leaning against the wall. "You're the one he can't let go of. I haven't even been in town much, but the other night at The Barn it was obvious how you affected him. We all see it. The whole world does, except you apparently."

Cassidy flopped onto the bed, tossing a sequined halter top into my lap. "This trip is supposed to be fun. So, stop overthinking everything. If Eero is who you want to be with, then go. Enjoy it."

"But you don't have to pretend, Nat," Ari said gently. "We get that there are still pieces you're not telling us. That's fine. But you don't have to carry them alone."

"We're here," Staci added. "Not just for the big stuff, but the little stuff too. Those things that make you feel like maybe you're too much to handle. You're not."

The sincerity in their voices made my throat tighten. I looked down at my half-packed suitcase, my hands fidgeting with a pair of sunglasses I didn't remember tossing in. "I guess I just feel like Eero's this great guy, right? On paper, he's perfect. And I like him. I do. But I'm not sure if I'm going with him because I want to or because I feel like I should."

Staci reached out and gave my hand a squeeze. "Then ask yourself: do you feel safe with him? Do you feel happy?"

I thought about that. The honest answer was I'm happy because not much is required of me. "Of course, I feel those things," I settled on. "Eero is a great guy."

"Then that's a good start," Ari said.

"And stop lying to yourself about Mitch not mattering," Cassidy added. "He does. Even if it's over."

I sighed. They weren't wrong, at least about the parts they knew about. But Mitch wasn't the only ghost haunting me. Racer wasn't on their radar, but he was still on mine. Circling, hovering, waiting for me to let my guard down...

"Go," Staci said, her voice softer now. "Let yourself have fun."

"Okay," I said. "I'll go. I'll try to enjoy it. But you guys keep an eye on things here. Like Marradine, if anyone calls. The university..."

"Don't worry. All your problems will be waiting for you

when you get back." Cassidy zipped up my duffle like she was putting an exclamation mark at the end of her sentence.

Staci wrapped an arm around me, pulling me into a gentle squeeze. "And when you come back, we'll still be here too."

"Thanks," I said, and it felt like I locked myself into this journey. There was no turning back now.

TEN

CALIFORNIA ISN'T ALL JUST palm trees and beach. That was always the impression I had growing up in Buffalo. I realized in the four years I'd been in California I'd never actually witnessed a snowfall here. I also found that cold weather was something you could get out of the habit of experiencing.

So, there I was sitting on an oversized couch in a super cozy cabin tucked against a ski slope in Big Bear. The cabin was quiet except for the crackle of the fire in the massive stone fireplace and the occasional groan of the old wood beams as the wind picked up outside. Snow dusted the windowsills and covered the ground in a blanket of white. It was peaceful and picturesque.

Despite the roaring fire and the heat turned up to seventy-two, I still felt the need to dress like an Eskimo. Long johns and a big fluffy white fleece sweatshirt Cassidy insisted I pack. Across from me in the kitchen, Eero went about making hot chocolate. His shirt was off, revealing the slightest glimmer of perspiration coating his perfectly sculpted pecs. I would think he'd be warm-blooded, too, given he grew up one Spanish beaches. Then again, he was sort of a showman. He had this hyper-energy vibe to him, a temperament that seemed to make sense that he was one of the fastest freestyle sprinters in the world.

"You're quiet, Love" he said, dropping a couple marshmallows in each of our mugs. "You thinking about something in particular?"

The word "love" hit me funny, but I didn't react. He used that a lot when talking to girls. More as punctuation than a term of endearment. "I was thinking about practicing next week," I lied. "I mean I know I can't with the team, but I still want to stay in the pool. Maybe work on my backstroke. It's been my weakest lately."

"You have the three top fastest times in the world in all IM distances this year without even trying. You're fine."

I shrugged. "Always room for improvement."

Eero set our mugs on the coffee table and sank onto the couch beside me. He stretched his long legs out in front of him and nudged my knee with his. "So, tell me really what's up. I'm listening, I promise."

His accent softened the quick cadence of his words. I wrapped my hands around the mug and stared into the dark liquid, letting the warmth seep into my palms. "Just... everything."

Eero nodded, his gaze steady. "You're carrying a lot. Have you thought about maybe lightening your load?"

"What do you mean? It's already pretty light now. I don't have school to worry about anymore."

"But what about the Dunes? Maybe that's something you can back off on, too. At least for a while."

I gave him a small smile. Sometimes I wasn't sure he fully understood "recovery." It could be his culture, but there was a part of me that wondered if he was just insensitive. In my three years sober, I'd been around booze and drugs at college parties and for the most part I hadn't been tempted. I credited that to good practice and support, but sometimes I wondered if Eero just figured I was "over it." It seemed too much to explain, and on some level, I thought maybe it would fall on deaf ears. Also, there were other anxious feelings I was trying really hard to get past.

He reached over, brushing a stray strand of hair behind my ear. The gesture was tender, almost too much so, and I felt a familiar tension coil in my chest. "It's nice you like to work with your old friends at that place but maybe you should focus on more positive and uplifting things now. Enjoy your new life. Have some fun."

"Like you do?" I teased, trying to keep the mood light.

His smile was easy, but there was an intensity in his eyes that made it clear he wasn't joking. "You know," he said after a moment, "I've been thinking about training for the Olympics."

I looked at him, pretending to be surprised. "Really?"

He nodded. "I was thinking that maybe it could be something we do together. Push each other, support each other. We're good as a team, Nat. We've always been good as a team."

It wasn't like I hadn't thought about a legit, world stage comeback. Reporters asked every time they saw me. Coaches called. Even old teammates and managers reached out now and then. Swimming was my first love. Maybe the only one I'd ever really known. Of course I missed it. Of course I wondered. But just because you loved something, it doesn't mean it loved you back.

Not after everything.

"Natalie?"

I blinked, bringing myself back to the conversation. "That sounds intense," I said, carefully noncommittal.

Eero laughed, a low, warm sound that filled the room. "Life

is intense. But it's also worth it. That's what I'm telling you. Have fun, enjoy."

He shifted closer, his knee brushing mine again. This time, he didn't pull away. "You know, back in Spain, life is simpler. No one is obsessed with perfection the way people are here. My family, we take things as they come. My dad always says, 'Do what feels good, and the rest will follow.'"

"That explains a lot about you," I stammered, trying to relax as his hand traveled up my thigh.

He grinned. "It's not a bad way to live. I try not to stress about the future too much. Focus on the moment, you know? Like this." He gestured to the fire, the snow outside, the two of us sitting together. "How could this not feel good?"

"Not everyone can be so relaxed," I said, shaking my head. "Some of us have things to prove."

Eero's smile faded slightly, and his gaze softened. "To whom? Your coaches? The media? Yourself?"

I didn't answer. His words hit too close to home, and I didn't want to unpack them, not here, not now.

"Nat," he said gently, leaning in again. "You don't have to prove anything to me. I already know how incredible you are."

His hand slipped up my arm, gentle but firm, as if grounding me to the moment. My first instinct was to pull away, to retreat into the safety of my own walls. But I hesitated, caught between the comfort of his touch and the fear of what it might mean.

"Eero," I began, my voice barely above a whisper. "I don't know if I can give you what you want."

His brow furrowed, but he didn't let go. "What do you think I want?"

"Something more than this," I said, gesturing vaguely between us. "Something I'm not sure I can give."

He was quiet for a long moment, his gaze searching mine.

"I'm not asking for anything, Nat. I just want you to let me in. Even if it's just a little."

His fingers lightly curled around mine. It was such a simple gesture, but it felt impossibly heavy. "I'm trying," I said finally. "I really am."

He nodded, his expression softening. "I told you before that I know what you've been through. I mean, I understand…"

The inflection of his voice and the way he looked at me told me he meant what happened with Racer. "Thanks, it's just something I'm still processing."

"I know." He touched his lips to mine. We'd made out before, and each time I would mentally talk myself into enjoying it a little more. It wasn't that I wasn't attracted to him, I was. Or that my body didn't respond, it did. I just wasn't sure that I liked that response. But I leaned into it anyway, with my eyes sealed shut in hyper-focus, and let his fingers linger on my cheek. He pushed against me, gently easing me against the over-stuffed pillows. My heart lurched. My breath caught…

When I splayed a shaky hand on his chest, Eero paused. I opened my eyes and Eero looked back at me with his brow raised in concern. "You okay, Love?"

I scanned the room making sure I was still in the cozy non-threatening cabin in the woods and not whatever horror I was conjuring in my own mind. "I'm fine," I blurted, weirdly stroking the smooth skin of his chest. "I'm just…"

I had no idea how to finish that sentence, so I didn't. Instead, I simply sat up and gulped my hot chocolate like it was a shot of whiskey.

"I'm not pushing you, am I?"

"No, and I really don't want to talk about it."

So, we sat there in silence for a while, the fire crackling softly in the hearth. Not sure for how long, a few minutes, maybe an hour. At some point Eero got up, put on a t-shirt, poured himself a glass of champagne, and hooked up his PlayStation. Call of Duty, his favorite. This is what we did most nights anyway when we hung out alone. After the small talk fizzled, the food and drink consumed, and we'd exhausted all other distractions, we'd resort to this. Him with a stranglehold on his controller while I played my own game in my head, watching the bombs explode on the screen.

———

Hours later, the fire in the living room had burned low to just embers and I was running on autopilot. Whatever momentum had carried us through the evening had evaporated into grey silence. Eero seemed to pick up what I was laying down...or wasn't in this case. But to his credit, he didn't push or pout.

We headed to bed.

The bedroom looked like something out of a Hallmark movie. Those Christmas ones where everyone drank warm cider and fell in cheesy love at some New England bed and breakfast. Vaulted ceilings, old pine beams, a massive sleigh bed piled with pillows and a thick down snow-white comforter. It had a fireplace of its own too, so Eero lit a small one to fall asleep to. It was cozy. Romantic. Staged to enhance a mood. My dysfunction, however, proved stronger than its vibe. Eero was asleep before I even changed into my pajamas, and I just ended up feeling like a failure.

I'd never actually slept in a bed with Eero before. Crashed on couches near him, sure. Napped during team retreats, yes. But this was different. This was intentional. I lay stiff as a board on my side of the bed, tucked under the blanket like it was body armor, careful to stay as far from him as possible without risking a tumble onto the floor. I could feel the heat from his body, but I didn't dare move closer. My thoughts drifted, weightless and slow. The warmth of the bed dulled the sharp edges of my mind, and for a moment, I almost believed I could rest.

But somewhere between an inhale and an exhale, something shifted.

The air thickened. The quiet deepened.

And then...

The hallway was long. Hot and dark but the walls glowed in a sickly yellow. I had no shoes. The floor was soft underfoot, damp almost. A hand touched my back, not rough but claiming. I turned.

Racer.

I didn't look at his face. I never could in dreams. Just glimpses. An elbow, a jawline, a smirk in profile. Too much shadow.

The door beside us opened by itself. I knew what was coming. The room was humid and humming. The TV blinked silent cartoons, colors too bright, too fast. Blue, red, green, repeat. There was a bed. Always a bed.

I didn't want to go in but there wasn't a choice. Never a choice. The door closed behind me with a click. The lock. The fucking lock. The room smelled like dust and sweat and all the times he'd done this to me before. The air pressed down like a heavy wet sheet...

His voice came from all directions at once. "You're fine."

The shadows on the wall leaned in closer. The bed creaked.

Hands...one, then another. The walls closed in. My vision blurred like static. My body melted into the dirty mattress under me. Then weight...on me, in me, overtaking me. A thousand invisible eyes blinked from the corners of the darkness. Laughing, low and sinister.

"She's not even fighting."

"She wants this. They always want this."

I tried to scream, but I had no voice. His breath was in my ear. His words coiled around my neck. The bed moaned under the pressure of something I couldn't push away.

"Natalie."

The word was distant at first, muffled, like underwater.

"Natalie, hey, wake up."

A hand on my shoulder.

I flinched violently, heart lurching into my throat as I scrambled upright, nearly knocking the lamp from the nightstand. The room spun. My breath came in short, choked gasps.

"Hey...hey, it's okay," Eero said, forcefully but with a crack in his voice that told me he didn't even believe his own words. He held his hands up; palms open like I was a wild animal he didn't want to spook. "It's me. It's just me."

The fire had burned almost completely out, so I stared wide-eyed into the darkness. Shadows clung to the corners of the room like ghosts and I shook my head trying to find words to send them away but...

"It's okay," he said again, gently this time, not moving closer. "You were having a nightmare."

I brought my knees up to my chest, arms locked around them like a shield. My throat burned as a sob clawed its way up, but I swallowed it down hard. I didn't cry. That wasn't something I did in front of people. Not even when it hurt.

Especially not when it hurt.

"I'm okay now," I managed. A blatant lie of course, but what wasn't one at this point? "I'm sorry to wake you."

Eero tried again to move toward me, slow and careful. He didn't try to pull me into his arms, didn't force anything. Just placed a hand lightly on my back, resting there like an anchor.

"I'm here," he said softly. "Whatever it was, it's not real."

But it *was* real. That's what made it so impossible to explain. I lay back down on my pillow facing away from him, trying like hell to stifle the tears and to keep my body from shaking. "I'm sorry," I whispered, the words fractured and ugly in my mouth. "I didn't mean to..."

"Don't," he said, making small circles with his hand on my back. "Don't apologize. You don't have to."

I felt him get up from the bed. The light in the bathroom snapped on and I heard the water running in the sink. Next thing I knew, he'd returned with a glass of water that I drank down in a few large gulps.

"Better?" he asked hopefully as I settled back down.

I felt like an even bigger spectacle thanks to the bathroom light he left on. I hated how small I felt. How *seen* I was. "This is embarrassing. I'm not usually..." I started, trying to lame-ass explain.

"It's okay, Love. Really."

The silence between us stretched, but this time it wasn't suffocating. He lay down beside me and I rolled over to face him. I wished I could understand his expression. Not judgment, but something close. Fear, maybe. Or confusion. A look that said, "I want to say the right thing right now, but I have no idea what that is."

I let myself lean into him just a little. With my head against his shoulder, my breath came easier. My tension released. It had to, right? Nothing could be that relentless for that long.

Maybe tomorrow I'd regret this. Letting my guard down simply because I was too tired in the moment to hold it haphazardly up. But I was a competitor. I was a survivor. I'd beat this. This...event. Maybe I'd pretend it never happened, shove it into that growing box of things I hadn't dealt with yet.

But for now, I just let Eero hold me.

And pretend I didn't wish he was someone else.

ELEVEN

"SO DID YOU SLEEP WITH HIM?"

Tillie eyed me from the other side of her desk rolling a pencil between her fingers. In the almost four years she'd been my therapist, she'd never been subtle. I loved that about her. No bullshit from her end which made it okay for her to call me out on mine.

"What do you think?" I asked knocking the verbal ball back over the net.

"That's what I want you to tell me."

I rolled my eyes. "There's nothing to tell. We were only there a night, and the opportunity never really presented itself anyway."

"Did the opportunity not present itself or were you trying hard to avoid it?"

I hated how logical that sounded. I stared at the flickering flame of the lavender candle that burned between us on her blotter.

"Don't get me wrong. I'm not pushing you into a sexual relationship," she assured me. "I'm just making sure you're not running scared from intimacy. It's okay to feel things."

I thought about Eero's smile. I liked how it was easy, cool. No intensity at all. I ran the pad of my fingers over my lips remembering the sensation of his kiss. I liked kissing him, or I probably would if everything was...normal again. If I was normal. "I want to feel things," I told her honestly. "I'm trying really hard."

"This isn't something you force, you know. What Racer did to you..."

"I know," I cut her off. It was strange but I figured as time went on, "The Racer Stuff" would be easier to deal with. But it seemed as though the more people brought it up or wanted to talk about it, the harder it was to contain in my head. I couldn't tuck it way in the dark recesses of my brain because it seemed everyone wanted access to it. Why couldn't it all just disappear?

"So," she tried again. This time she spoke softer, as if I was some broken child. "Can you please tell me all about your trip? Just the trip."

I shifted in my seat. PG details like what I ate and the route we took to get there I could handle. I took a deep breath and tucked my legs underneath me. "It was nice. Quiet. Eero found this cabin right by the lake, and it snowed the whole time. It felt like being in a snow globe."

Tillie smiled faintly. "Sounds picturesque."

"It was." I hesitated, my fingers fidgeting with the seam of my jeans. "See...Eero...he's good at making things feel simple. Like it's okay to just be in the moment. But I don't think I'm built that way."

"Why not?" Tillie asked gently.

I let out a small laugh, shaking my head. "Because I'm more of the 'deep focus' type. I've spent my whole life chasing something. Approval, medals, redemption. It's hard to just switch that off."

"You're not a machine, Natalie," Tillie said firmly. "You

don't have to run at full speed all the time. In fact, it's not sustainable. You know that."

"Yeah, well, try telling that to the rest of the world," I muttered. "And I've been thinking about Annie a lot lately."

The room grew quiet. I suddenly became aware of the spa music playing in the background. And presumably the whole time we'd been sitting there. I was pretty sure that I still hadn't worked through Annie's death from leukemia three years earlier. She was my swim team partner and best friend. We pushed each other and motivated each other in the best possible way. "I didn't reapply to school," I heard myself say. "So that also means I'm not swimming anymore because I'm permanently off the team. So no NCAA title defense, no prep for international competition. Just done."

I let that revelation simmer around us. Give it the moment of silence it deserved.

"I haven't been in a pool in weeks anyway," I continued. "The last time I went this long I was here at the Dunes...or on my back in Racer's trailer."

When there was no response to that, I looked up. To Tillie's credit her expression was the same. Warm, open, no judgment. I both loved and hated that. Any swim coach I ever had would treat me to a verbal kick in the ass for that kind of breach of self-discipline. I responded well to that in the past, for the most part. Other than it sending me into a spiral of addiction and rehab.

"What happened do you think?" Tillie asked. "I thought you were doing well."

She was working up to something. I'd been in this room long enough to know when Tillie was laying groundwork for a deeper dig. And I had a sinking suspicion I knew where it was headed.

"Is this where you ask me about Mitch?" I said, not quite defensive, but not open either.

Her expression didn't change, but something about the vibe did. "I wasn't going to force it," she said gently. "But I do think there's something there. Not necessarily about him, but about what Mitch brings up for you, in situations like this weekend. Especially in contrast to Eero."

"Mitch knows pretty much every gory detail of what happened with Racer. Although doesn't everyone? The asshole sold videos of what he did to me, and as it turns out, the rest of the girls he violated. Remember how the tabloids were all over the case?"

"I remember," she assured me. "Mitch is in a unique position in that he's a professional who deals with that type of thing."

"That's the thing. I didn't want him to 'deal with me,'" I used air quotes. "I wanted him to forget it."

Tillie offered a knowing smile. "That's the thing, you can't. You shouldn't, and all your efforts in trying to do so are pushing you in a direction you don't want to be going in. Mitch knows that."

"I just feel like when I left the Dunes I had answers. I had confidence. Everyone kept telling me if I just stayed sober and worked on myself, I'd be able to make better decisions. But there're so many things that keep happening to me that I have no control over. There're no decisions to be made."

"You mean you can't help the way you feel." Tillie clarified.

"Right now I'm just super pissed." I covered my face with my hands and took a deep breath. "I'm pissed that my best friend is gone. I'm pissed that I've seriously fucked up college and my swim career. One I was lucky enough to have a second chance at, by the way. But the biggest thing that makes me so uncontrollably livid is that I've let Racer ruin every aspect of my life. Me! I let it happen then, and I keep letting it happen now!"

"That was not your fault, Natalie!" Tillie said with a steel in her voice that startled me. "That was in NO WAY YOUR FAULT!" She stabbed her stubby finger on her blotter to emphasize every word.

"But at some point, I'm responsible for how I deal with it, aren't I?" I sat up to the desk and moved the candle between us so I could look Tillie deeper in the eyes. "Eero thinks I should consider training for the Olympics."

Tillie's eyes lifted slightly. Not surprised, just curious. "Do you think you should?"

I gave a dry laugh. "I mean...on paper, it sounds insane, right? My whole life's a dumpster fire. And he's like, 'Why not the Olympics?'"

Her smile was subtle. "Sometimes outside perspective has its uses."

"Yeah. Maybe." I paused. "The thing is it didn't sound totally insane. Not when he said it. It was weird. Like for a second, if I didn't overthink it, I could actually see it. Me, training again. Focused. Strong."

"And how did that feel?" she asked.

I hesitated. "Like I remembered who I was for a second. Like I could breathe."

Tillie nodded slowly. "Because swimming has always been your anchor. It's how you've measured yourself; structured your world."

"Exactly," I said. "There's this girl on the swim team. Paris. She's cocky and driven and really talented. I hate her and respect her all at once. But for whatever reason when she's around, the competitive instinct kicks in."

Tillie scribbled something in her notebook before meeting my gaze again. "Do you think Paris gets to you because she's reflecting back something you see in yourself?"

The question caught me off guard, and I leaned back in my chair, staring at the ceiling. "Maybe all of it," I admitted after a long pause. "She's like this mirror of everything I hate about myself. The insecurity, the need to prove something, the fear of not being enough. And she just amplifies it."

"That's a lot to carry," Tillie said softly. "But sometimes mirrors can be helpful. You ever think that's why you want to help Marradine so much?"

The thing was, I did feel this strong pull to help her. I realized no one really ever asked me to. I just took it upon myself when she got to the Dunes that we could relate. Both of us being in the public eye, and hell, we were both found passed out on the floor before we got here. "I just want to be useful, I guess."

"You're allowed to set boundaries, Natalie," she said finally. "With Eero, with Paris, with everyone. You can still chase your goals without losing yourself in the process."

I nodded slowly, her words sinking in. "Boundaries," I repeated, as if testing the word. "I'll think about it."

Tillie leaned forward just slightly, elbows resting on the edge of her desk. "Natalie, if swimming's the thing that still feels like home, then it's worth exploring. Not because Eero said it, not because the world wants your comeback, but because you're allowed to want something that makes you feel alive again."

I didn't say anything. I wasn't sure I could. But a small part of me, the part that hadn't been drowned out by fear, or grief, or shame, was nodding along with her. For the first time in a long while, it didn't feel impossible. "I'm gonna seriously think about it."

When she closed her notebook, I knew head-shrinking time was over and then it was just us two girls shooting the shit. She pulled out two grape seltzer waters from the minifridge and handed one to me. "Are you gonna stop over to the residence halls and see Marradine today?"

I shrugged. "Hadn't planned on it. I figured she needed a break from me. Hell, I need a break from me."

"I'm sure she's thankful for your friendship," Tillie said. "And I'm pretty sure no one else can relate to her like you can. Public eye. Pressure."

"I just can't fathom keeping my mouth shut all this time."

Tillie laughed. "You're both finding your voices now, aren't you?"

I considered the question and was thankful that our session was over because I really didn't want to answer it.

———

The day after my meeting with Tillie, I headed to the gallery with Staci. Ari had flown out to Nevada for the week, and Lance was buried in donor meetings and client deadlines. That left the auction prep grunt work to us. The big Valentine's Day gala was just a month away. I loved we decided to host it exactly on February 14th...Annie had always been a sucker for sentiment.

Around us, a dozen or so paintings were propped against the white walls of the lobby, waiting to be cataloged. Moody. Some borderline erotic. Staci went from piece to piece with a note pad and pencil assigning numbers and conjuring up fancy descriptions for them. I stood there holding an iPad, mostly useless.

"I feel like a kid tagging along to her mom's job," I muttered. "Like I need a coloring book and crayons or something."

Staci laughed. "I know you're joking, but your name's half the reason we're getting these pieces. Might not be your taste, but it's good for the foundation and Lance's gallery."

"Yeah. I guess."

She was in full manager mode now. Black blazer, slick ponytail, platform boots. Meanwhile, I wore my usual Could-Be-A-College-Kid but Also-Could-Be-Homeless uniform: baggy jeans and a grey T-shirt, hair up in a messy bun.

"That one's going to give someone nightmares," I said, nodding toward a dark oil painting of a faceless ballerina collapsing on stage. "I'm not an art critic, but shouldn't this stuff be more...I don't know, less horrifying?"

Staci didn't look up from her notes. "What do you want, puppies and picnics? That piece is expected to pull ten grand. Try not to insult the merchandise."

"I'm not insulting it," I said. "I'm just observing it."

I glanced at the spreadsheet clipped to Staci's clipboard. The next piece was titled *Untethered Grace,* a girl with wild eyes, long black hair, and a torn white dress, sword-fighting a horse. *Untethered Song* showed the same girl running through a forest with a flute. Two more featured her, too. Same girl, same vibe. Vivid. Cryptic. Unsettling.

"I don't get why these four are so different from the rest." I asked. "They just seem more...intense."

"Those are from Damian Cross' collection," she explained. "And you' re right. They're way different than any other of the pieces his estate donated."

"It's like they're telling a story or something."

Staci took a step back, eyeing the canvas of the last one *Untethered Night.* The dark-haired girl hiding in a house on fire. "Maybe that's the point. A good collection shows range."

"A genius can have many moods," came a smooth, genial voice from behind us.

We both turned.

Karl Rollings strolled in with the unhurried confidence of someone who owned the joint. He wore a navy suit and sported a leather portfolio tucked neatly under one arm. His salt-and-pepper hair was slicked back, and his smile was warm in the way mastered by brand reps and con artists.

"Ladies," he said with a soft nod. "Everything coming together all right?"

Staci straightened, offering a polite hand. "Mr. Rollings. Thanks again for coordinating the shipment. Everything arrived perfectly."

"Glad to hear it. Damian cared deeply about creative expression, being such a prolific filmmaker himself. His art collection was a prized possession of his. He used to say every canvas was a conversation the artist hadn't finished."

I glanced at a nearby piece, an ethereal mermaid wearing a gas mask floating through clouds. Whatever conversation that was, I wondered if it was chemically enhanced.

Karl nodded to a painting of a yellow serpent coiled in a rose garden. "Some of these are a little... perverse," he said, like it was a word he reluctantly settled on. "But Damian did have a fondness for that kind of thing. Sometimes I wonder if it's what got him killed."

Staci gave me a subtle look, unsure how to respond. "Everyone's heard rumors," she said carefully. "But who really knows what drives a person?"

Karl smiled faintly. "We all want to assign meaning to things once someone's gone. Tragedy makes critics of us all."

There was a pause. Deliberate. Uncomfortable. Then...

"And how is our young friend Marradine, over at the Dunes?"

His shift in subject was so abrupt it felt like being yanked off a stage. "How did you know she was there?" I asked. "Her location's supposed to be confidential."

"Holly Inez mentioned it. She also said you were one of her approved visitors. Small world." He shrugged lightly. "I always liked the girl. She had a wild side that worked against her but spent an awful lot of time by herself in Damian's stables. She loved the horses, I guess."

He turned his eyes back to the serpent painting.

"I suppose if it was her who killed him," he said, almost absentmindedly, "maybe it was justified."

My pulse ticked up. "Marradine is doing fine. Considering."

"That's all anyone's doing these days. Considering." He chuckled softly. "Gossip spreads faster than truth. One minute you're a muse, the next you're a suspect."

"If you're insinuating Marradine had something to do with Damian's death..."

"Oh, no," he said, hands raised. "Of course not. I'm just saying quiet people hide big stories. And that's fine, but stories can have consequences."

He let that sit for a moment. Staci shifted beside me, arms crossed now.

"I'm only here to ensure everyone involved in this event is seen in the best possible light," he said smoothly. "You, Natalie. Your friend, Annie. And of course, to a lesser extent, Damian." He took one final look around the room, then nodded. "If there's anything you need, truly, don't hesitate."

And with that, he turned and walked out. Calm. Polished. Like we'd just had a chat about the weather. Staci and I watched him through the glass as he lit a cigarette, climbed into a silver BMW and pulled away.

The gallery was silent for a long moment.

"He's a douchebag," Staci muttered.

"Noted," I agreed. "But you know what scares me?"

She turned. "What?"

"I think Marradine might know what happened that night. I'm just not sure she remembers."

Staci didn't say anything for a moment. When she did, her voice was quiet. "Then let's hope if and when she does, she tells someone who deserves to hear about it."

———

I found Marradine on the patio behind the main lounge, sitting cross-legged on the stone ledge with her ever-present notebook in her lap. This was a favorite spot for me, too, when I was at the Dunes. It was shaded and private and if you positioned yourself just at the right spot, you had a gorgeous view of the gardens and the mountains as a backdrop. The Dunes wasn't all bad. It was peaceful. Relaxing. How crazy was it that more and more lately, I found myself nostalgic, even homesick for my long days back here at rehab.

She had pen to paper, per her usual, and she looked pretty content with that. Her caramel hair fell in tendrils from a loose bun and she wore a white t-shirt and khakis. The uniform for the first of the five levels of residents here. She didn't look up when I approached. Just paused for a beat, then scribbled something and held the notebook out toward me.

"Sorry it's been a minute. I was unpacking from my big trip," I kidded.

She smirked and rolled her eyes then gestured toward the words on the page.

So did he want to sleep with you?

I blinked. "Wow. How long have you been waiting to ask me that?"

Marradine didn't smile, but her eyes had that glint. She wasn't asking to gossip. She was asking to understand.

"Yes, we shared a bed. No, nothing happened."

She tilted her head, pen ready again.

Nothing?

I figured my embarrassing nightmare didn't qualify as newsworthy. "I don't think I'm built for romance right now," I admitted.

She nodded, then wrote:

That Racer guy did a number on you, huh?

I weirdly appreciated her bluntness. It made me feel understood. Sometimes when I chatted with her, I felt like I was talking to myself.

"Yeah, Racer did mess me up pretty bad. I mean, I figured since I couldn't remember much of what he did, it wouldn't matter. But now I can. And it does."

She nodded again, slow and empathetic. Then handed me her pad once more.

You okay? Maybe sometimes it's better not to remember.

"I thought that, too," I said. "I guess sometimes I still think that, but I can't unknow it now."

We sat in silence for a while, letting the warmth of the sun settle around us.

Trying to change the subject, I shifted gears. "So now that I'm back," I said lightly, "I can finally focus on the auction. We've all been acting like it's just another event, but it's for Annie. It feels different. I want it to be something that would've made her proud."

At the mention of Annie, Marradine's expression softened.

"Staci's got most of the catalog organized," I continued. "Some of the pieces are moody and weird, but beautiful. I meant to tell you, Karl Rollings, Damian Cross' attorney, donated a small set from Damian's estate. Four paintings. It was really generous of him to think of the foundation."

That's when I saw it.

Her whole body shifted. Not dramatically, but enough. Like someone had pulled a string tight inside her. Her spine straightened. Her chin lifted. She clutched her notebook like it was the only thing tethering her to the ground.

"Marradine?" I asked quietly.

But she was already on her feet, notebook hugged tight to her chest.

"Wait, did I say something wrong?"

Just as she vanished around a corner, a nurse in soft blue scrubs walked by, pushing a cart of linens toward the east wing. She paused, watched Marradine go, then sighed and shook her head with a small, tired smile.

"She does that," she said, not unkindly. "Someone says something she doesn't like, and poof. Wall goes up, notebook shuts, she ghosts."

I raised an eyebrow. "That happen a lot?"

"All the time. The other day a girl offered her a breath mint, and she locked herself in her room for three hours."

I tried to make light of it. "Maybe she thought it was code for 'you have bad breath.'"

"Still seemed like a big overreaction," the nurse said with a shrug, then continued on her way.

I stared after Marradine, a knot tightening in my stomach. Did I say something, or not say something? My phone buzzed in my lap.

A group text to basically everyone we knew from Staci lit up the screen:

Tomorrow. Sunset. Beach bonfire to celebrate our new forever roomie Cassidy! You're not allowed to say no. Bring snacks or be publicly shamed.

I exhaled, grateful for the distraction. Staci, ever on brand, bossy, sunny, and usually right. The idea of celebrating felt laughable with everything else looming. Mitch, the auction, Marradine, Eero. Still. Maybe pretending everything was amazing for one night wouldn't kill me.

Maybe.

TWELVE

WHEN I WOKE up Saturday to the clanking of dishes and running water, I assumed Lance and Staci were in mid-breakfast prep. They did that a lot. Functioned like normal people, I mean. They'd get up early, go for walks on the beach. Clean, pay bills, discuss politics. Couple stuff. They didn't wake up at 5:37 in the afternoon from naps that started at 11 a.m. and debate with themselves about the necessity of a shower and clean clothes. Which I realized was my current situation.

Today was Cassidy's beach party.

Fuck.

I hit the shower. That was one of the best things about the beach house was that all four bedrooms had their own bathroom. Swank. Staci's mom's extra-ness paid off for all of us in this instance. My own bathroom was key to my existence. I could drink water, do my business, shower, wash my clothes if I had to, without leaving the confines of my bedroom walls. Sometimes I wondered how long I could last in there, like a prisoner in solitary confinement. Or my own fallout shelter.

I'd become particular in how I bathed these days, too. I preferred to do so during the day with people at home. Bedroom and bathroom door had to be locked. I'd start the water but adjust it when I was already under it. Temperature didn't matter. Scalding hot and ice cold were both good for different reasons.

I'd stand there facing out of the glass, eyes fixed on the doorknob. The goal was to complete my mission before everything was so steamed up that I couldn't see out. I'd scrub and shave as fast as I could. Hair was washed twice a week. It was up most of the time, so greasiness didn't matter. I'd towel dry still standing in the shower. The drying part was most important. There was nothing worse than fabric sticking to damp skin. Then I'd step out, and dress in whatever baggy ensembles I found in the random clean clothes piles next to my desk.

Ten minutes. Tops.

"Oh good! You're alive!" Cassidy greeted me from the kitchen table wearing the new pink flamingo beach coverup Staci bought her for the big day. In front of her was an explosion of a third-grade art project. Markers, posterboard, streamers, glue sticks and even confetti that Cassidy kept throwing in the air. "How can you sleep so late when we have so much party to plan!" she asked.

Staci, Lance, Ari and even Janessa were all at the kitchen island looking up from whatever I'd distracted them from. There were cutting boards and bowls of fruit. Bricks of cheese and jars of dressing. Party food prep frenzy. I felt bad I wasn't participating. "You guys could have woken me up," I said. "I wanted to help set up."

"Don't worry. There's still a ton to do." Lance stood and brushed the chip dust from his hands. "You can take my spot in snack prep. I'm gonna go fill the coolers and you ladies can chat."

Lance left and I caught the vibe I walked in mid-convo. Not that I was a paranoid person but lately when I left or entered rooms, it felt like there was something I was missing. Ari sat next to Staci and took a long gulp from her Stanley. I could tell by the way she snapped the top shut she had something on her mind.

"What?" I asked.

"Do you always sleep this late?"

I looked at Staci for some direction. "No, not always." I grabbed the pitcher of orange juice from the fridge and poured myself a glass.

"But lately," Ari said. "At least when I'm in town."

"What, you think I'm avoiding you or something?" I laughed to signify an attempt at a joke, but it seemed no one else thought it was funny. "I've just been catching up on my sleep. Reset for the coming semester."

Ari nodded. "Oh, that's right. Classes started last week, didn't they?"

Here's the thing about former addicts. We're the best bullshit artists on the planet. We can also recognize it a mile away. These girls were no fools.

"I think you got something mental going on," Cassidy declared while she colored in the poster boarder with a purple Crayola.

"What do you mean, 'mental?'"

"Like something is not right in your head. You don't swim and you don't go to school. You don't sleep at night, and you dress like a homeless vampire."

"Is that all?"

She looked up at me and dramatically tossed her crayon back into the shoebox. "I think you're hiding something, Natalie. Crazy always recognizes crazy."

It sounded like both a warning and a declaration. It had been three years since I lived with her, and I was suddenly reminded never to underestimate Cassidy's perception, the crystal clarity that would randomly show itself in complex situations like this. Discounting her was useless. The best way to derail her was to distract.

"So, who is coming to this big blow out anyway?" I asked, watching as Staci meticulously drew *Cassidy's Beach Bonfire Welcome Bash* across a white banner with purple marker. I felt bad I was out of the loop on this since I'd been so busy keeping up the appearance of my farce of a life. I hadn't even been privy to any kind of guest list.

"Everyone we know," Cassidy said happily. "I want to show the world how much I've evolved."

Cassidy reached around me for the real remote and pointed to the great room television on the wall. Since the wildfires a few months back, we'd become accustomed to not making any concrete outdoor plans until Channel 8's BriteWeather meteorologist Sally Hill gave us the "all clear." As far as I could see, there wasn't a single cloud to block the beautiful setting sun, but of course any excuse for Cassidy to park her ass in front of the TV. She'd find it. "I really like all the news channels here," she said, furiously pushing the "up" button on the volume. "That's when I knew that Los Angeles could truly be my home."

Top of the hour, headline news. Government scandals, assorted diseases, Lakers recap. I picked up my third cucumber and placed it strategically on the cutting board. My knife poised on its flesh. And then...

"Today in Buffalo, New York, Roger 'Racer' Jameson... human trafficking...Natalie Collins..."

Shit!

I snatched my finger out from under the knife's blade. Drops of blood dribbled down my hand and over the row of sliced cucumbers. I grabbed a napkin from the little holder in front of me and held it tight on my wound.

Everyone turned laser focused on the screen. Ginger Phillips, a talking head I'd come to like now totally betrayed me, revealing all the dirty details of everything I wanted to forget. Why the hell would a Los Angeles newscast give a shit about some pervert clear across the country? Especially when they had their own home-grown scandal like the Damian Cross case here?

When Ginger mercifully shut the fuck up, all eyes again swung in my direction. I clenched my sliced finger tighter then realized I'd bled through the napkin. I grabbed another one from the holder and wrapped it around.

"Wait a minute. Did you know Racer's sentencing was going on in Buffalo?" Staci asked, like a mother getting to the bottom of her troubled child's transgression. "Is this what's been setting you off lately?"

I wasn't sure whether to be defensive or flattered by her concern. I settled on "incredulous and oblivious" by her observation. "What are you talking about? What do I care about what goes on with all that? That's all behind me."

"Is it?" Janessa added. "I don't know all the particulars but if it's a victim impact hearing like the news just said, wouldn't you be like, the star witness?"

"That's the thing, I didn't witness anything. Why would they want me there?"

"But you're like the key to their case," Ari said. "Wouldn't they need you to testify?"

I rolled my eyes. "It's not a trial," I argued. "There wasn't one, remember? This is all just meaningless bullshit. The lady said he'll go to jail. The end. That's it."

"So, you *did* know about this hearing thing?" Staci asked.

Lance came through the door, wiping his hands on a dish cloth. "Wait, is that why your mom has been calling you and sending all that mail? Is that why you don't want to talk to her?"

So, it wasn't just Cassidy who'd been clocking my time. Everyone was on to me. When had I gotten so sloppy at covering my tracks? I used to be so stealth. "Look, I told you guys. Whatever the bullshit is going on in Buffalo, it stays in Buffalo. I'm here. We are ALL here so it's not even any of our businesses."

"I can tell by your left nostril flaring that you're not even buying what you're saying." Cassidy argued. "Why should we?"

Cassidy stared me down with narrowed eyes and her skinny bare arms folded against her. She was no pushover. I reminded myself she may be a sweetheart now, but there was a time she'd knocked over convenience stores with metal shivs.

"Because I'm telling you the truth," I insisted.

We all jumped when the sliding glass door opened. Eero stepped inside looking bonfire festive in his khaki cargos shorts and a Hawaiian shirt carrying a case of Imported beer. "What's going on?" he greeted, but with the inflection of an actual question.

He looked at me, then the others, then back again. My sliced finger throbbed under the paper napkin. Fortunately, my friends respected my boundaries. The "Racer Thing" was a "Pre- Eero" issue. They wouldn't open their mouths unless I did first.

I wasn't going to.

"I cut my finger open," I blurted, holding up my bloody stump as proof.

He chuckled and leaned down to kiss my cheek. "You okay? You really are bad at cooking, aren't you?"

"Do we have Band-Aids?" I asked no one in particular.

"In your bathroom medicine cabinet," Cassidy said, still scowling at me. "In between your pink toothbrush and the super absorbent tampons." She snatched up her banner and walked outside to the deck table.

"What's her problem?" Eero said with a chuckle. "You'd think she'd be in a better mood if her friends were throwing her a party."

"Who knows," I answered before anyone else could. I stood and headed toward my room for Band-Aids. I was already digging through my medicine cabinet when Eero slipped his hand gently over my shoulder.

"Hey, did something happen? You seemed off when I walked in here and everyone looked really pissed off?"

"No, nothing happened. Just you know, girl stuff." When I waved the tampon box in his face, I figured that would disarm him. It didn't.

"You know you can tell me things, right? Like it takes a lot for me to get mad about anything. Whatever it is, I'm sure it's no big deal."

"You're right," I said. "It's no big deal. Just party planning logistics."

He looked pleased with himself and ran his hands down my arms. "I've been worried about you, ya know. I just want you to be happy."

"Just keep doing what you do best. Showing me a good time." I kissed him softly for good measure. Well strategized. A transaction, if you will. I feed you bullshit; you accept it.

"Sounds good," he said with a smile and pinched my cheek. "Maybe you can let out that frustration with a beach volleyball game. My suitemates are coming and they're looking for a real competition. You in?"

Before I could respond he let out a whoop and headed back out to the kitchen. People were showing up now. I could hear his laughter over the buzz of conversation outside. The Band-Aid wrapper crinkled in my hand. I peeled it open and pressed it to my finger. It was fine. I was fine. There was a party after all and all I had to do was show up

---

When I finally stepped out onto the deck, I'd just missed the sunset. Lance moved along the perimeter of the beach, lighting Tiki torches one by one, their flames flickering to life like little sentinels guarding the shoreline. The bonfire crackled at the far end of the sand in a special concrete pit because laws in Southern California are pretty strict. Overhead, strands of silver lights crisscrossed the deck lighting the place up like midday. Calypso beats rolled from the speakers. It smelled like BBQ and ocean salt. Everything was perfect and yet all I could feel was the strain in my shoulders, the pull in my stomach, and the way my pulse picked up as I tried to convince myself I wanted to be there.

"You get that to stop bleeding finally?" Staci asked over my shoulder. She wore a purple sun dress and her hair in two braids Pippi Longstocking style. She carried a platter of cut-up fruit and little toothpicks in bamboo cups. Cassidy ran by and stole a chuck of pineapple.

"Yeah, that's what took me so long to get dressed." I told her, watching Cassidy happily run out to the sand. "I didn't want to get blood all over my clothes."

"Don't think anybody would have noticed." She gave me a curious once-over. Clearly, she did not love the baggy black on black t-shirt and shorts ensemble. "You couldn't have worn something more festive?"

"We're in the dark, aren't we?"

Staci cocked her head like she was making a point. "Certainly looks that way, doesn't it?"

I surveyed the scene on the beach in front of me. About fifty people. Friends of Staci and Lance's though the gallery. Ari's flight attendant friends, Eeros suitemates, Janessa's sorority sisters. There were other Pepperdine people, too. For the most part, no one I really felt like being social with.

Staci returned with a can of ginger ale. She popped the top

and handed it to me. "So, I'm gonna ask one more time. Are you okay? You haven't been yourself and today with the news story on TV..."

"I'm fine," I assured her.

"Even Eero's a little worried about you. And he doesn't seem to worry much about anything."

"That's true," I agreed. "Listen, is everyone you invited here?"

Staci blew out a breath. "If you're asking me about Mitch, no he's not coming. He said he had some other function he couldn't get out of tonight."

"With Holly Inez?" It was more a statement than a question. "Do you think he's not here because of Eero?"

"I think Mitch would be here in a minute if he knew you wanted him to be."

"Hey Nat, can you go get more ice?" Lance yelled up at me from the beach. He held a load of driftwood and was heading in the direction of the bonfire. "After that what do you say we get our game of beach volleyball together? Cassidy's been asking."

I laughed. "When has she ever played it?"

"But you're sure you're okay?" Staci asked. "You would tell me, right? I mean you're not like..." she gulped. "You're not using or anything, are you?"

"Hey Natalie! Come on, you're on my team!" Eero stood by the volleyball net with a ball in his hand. I could tell by the way his shirt was off and tied on his head like a do-rag he meant business.

"No, of course I am not using," I whispered to Staci. At least that I could say that with certainty. "I promise, I'm not."

Staci smiled and I could tell she was relieved. "I'll grab the ice," she said. "You go play. You know how Cassidy is when you make her wait."

I stepped down from the deck and onto the sand, slipping

off my shoes as I went. The damp grit under my bare feet felt unsteady. Repulsive. I dug in, making little divots with my toes before making my way down to the net. Lance and his amped up gallery friends were already in position on one side, while Eero stood on ours, effortlessly cool with his hands on his hips.

Eero grinned. "Ah, finally. Our secret weapon arrives."

"I'm five feet tall and I'm injured." I waved my bandaged stump of a finger in the air. "I'm no secret weapon. I'm more of a liability."

"You'll do just fine," he said, offering a high five I half-heartedly returned. "Low expectations, high reward. It's the European way."

Cassidy blew her whistle; a plastic one she had tied to her wrist with a hair tie. She stood with Eero and me, convinced we were the winning team. "Let's go! We've got beach domination to achieve!"

"You ready?" Eero asked, his voice dropping just enough for only me to hear. He nudged my arm gently with his elbow. "Just have fun. No medals, no pressure."

"Right," I said, as I stepped into place. "Just fun."

"Your serve, Collins!" Staci called.

I caught the ball she lobbed over the net. The cool sand stuck to my palms, and I wiped them off on my shorts. Sweat trickled down my back. Goosebumps bloomed on my skin. My hair fell into my face. Strands tangled against my lips.

"Let's see it, Natalie!" Eero called behind me. "Show us what you got!"

I tossed the ball into the air, squinting up at the lavender sky. My fist met it hard and the ball shot across the net like a missile. Lance dove after it with a dramatic grunt, missed by a mile, and landed flat in the sand. Cassidy howled with laughter so hard she spilled her seltzer.

"That's my girl," Eero, cheered. "Keep going. Don't stop!"

I laughed, too. It was funny, or at least I wanted it to be. I wiped the moisture from my brow. One of Eero's friends. Nick? Nate? Strode by me. He had dark hair that brushed his shoulders and a crooked half-smile that tugged at the corner of his mouth. His arm grazed mine, his body tense and muscles flexed, breath uneven from exertion. And then, the scent.

Not identical, but close enough.

Cologne. Bitter citrus and ash. Thick. The kind that sank into skin, into sheets, into memories. It curled around me, sealing me inside it like a tomb. In the firelight, shirtless, faceless figures surrounded me. Dark shadows, advancing, ready to take what I was serving up. They closed in on me...laughed...teased... taunted.

Back in that room.

"We're ready for you girl! Let's see what you got!"

"Let's go, Nat! One more time!"

Eero handed me the ball and took my place at the line in the sand. Again, I served it up and it shot back towards me like a laser. I ran after it. Eero, Nick/Nate, me, our whole side dove for it. And then...a blur of motion. A crash. Something slammed into me and suddenly, I was flat in the sand.

Damn girl!

Breathless. Paralyzed. Stunned, numb and incoherent. His body on mine. The pressure. The weight. My skin burned. My throat closed but somehow I found my voice.

"GET OFF ME!!"

I shoved, hard. Nick/Nate jerked back, hands lifted in stunned surrender. "Natalie!"

"Leave me alone!" I was already up and moving, staggering to my feet with sand in my mouth and my arms trembling like I'd been hit by lightning. I bent forward, choking on air I couldn't seem to catch.

Staci's voice came from beside me, calm and steady. "Hey. Come walk with me, yeah?"

"Don't touch me!"

Her eyes met mine. Confusion, concern. Every inch of my skin buzzed like I'd been electrocuted. Everyone stared. Eero frozen in the sand, Cassidy hovering. I felt trapped but ready to make a break for it.

"Natalie, Love," Eero said softly. "You're okay, right?"

No. I most definitely was not.

I turned and ran across the sand, past the torches, up the steps. I didn't stop until I reached my bedroom, slammed the door, and locked it. My knees hit the floor, and I curled forward, arms wrapped tight around myself.

And I thought Buffalo had been the worst of it.

Not even close.

THIRTEEN

Dear Marradine
Who cares

Girl, I think you're on to something. When I first met you, I spent a lot of time thinking about how hard it must be not to talk. Ever. And not so much because I would miss idle conversation or socializing but simply because I really just like to put my two cents out there. But I have to say after what happened to me tonight, I'm not sure I have any "cents" left at all.

So there's this hearing thing I'm supposed to go to. It's what they call a victim impact statement that you give in a courtroom when your perpetrator is facing their sentencing. Somehow, how I feel about this asshole helps the judge decide how much time he spends in prison. That seems like a lot of pressure. Like if I don't paint a graphic enough picture or use enough adjectives, this guy can roam free in seven years instead of ten? Who fucking cares? What could I possibly say that this judge wouldn't already know? Read the tabloids from the past three years, Your Honor! Natalie Collins has lost her mind!

That's' all. I have no other words. Clearly, you're the best person in the world to understand that.

———

THAT NIGHT I ACTUALLY SLEPT. Or at least I passed out from exhaustion because when I woke up with the sun in my eyes, my whole body ached as if I'd run a marathon. There wasn't much I could remember about the night before, other than I made a complete asshole out of myself. Unfortunately, I couldn't blame it on pills or booze. Just a straight edge version of Natalie Collins doing what she did best. Public meltdown.

There was a knock on my bedroom door. I could tell by the soft knuckled strike it was Staci. I didn't answer. I just sat on the edge of my bed and held my breath.

She knocked again and then a careful voice from the other side. "Hey, Natalie? You're alive right? I mean, I can hear you moving around in there."

Could she? Damn these thin walls and my cloddish feet. My goal was to be so quiet that they would forget I existed, at least for a little while. Thanks to Cassidy's obsession with Survivor, I low-key developed a habit of stashing non-perishables in my room. As far as I could tell there wasn't a single reason to leave it for the next week or so. No one to see, nowhere to go and I was pretty sure I had a box of Pop-Tarts stashed somewhere in my desk.

Another knock. This time a playful staccato. "Girl, please come out and talk to me," Ari coaxed. "I leave for the airport in a few minutes, and I won't be back for a week. We can have a cup of coffee."

Coffee. That did sound good. My stomach made a noise. Hunger? Anxiety? Coffee would cure neither, which suited me fine. I didn't deserve to solve my own problems when I'd caused so many for everyone else.

Then came the knock I knew for sure was Cassidy. It sounded like she was rubbing the side of the door like somebody would rub one's back. "Natalie, please come out," came the weak shaky voice. "Lance brought donuts. The good kind you like, with the weird filling." A pause. "Please, Nat. Just come to the living room."

I didn't move. My legs felt like noodles. I didn't want to explain or make an excuse...

"I don't like when you're not strong, Natalie. It makes me feel scared."

Well shit, Cass.

When you put it that way...

I didn't bother to change even though I still sported my black sand-coated long sleeve t-shirt and shorts from the night before. My hair hung tangled and loose. My unbrushed teeth felt furry. My cheeks hurt like sunburn, but I knew that was the sting of dried tears. Screw it. Who was there to impress?

I stepped out the door and shuffled toward the living room like I was being tried in a courtroom. As it turns out, it might as well have been.

Because there they all were.

Staci sat on the couch in a lavender track suit, hands folded so tight in her lap her knuckles were white. Ari was next to her, dressed in her navy-blue flight attendant's uniform, a nervous smile pulling on her red lips. Janessa, who clearly came straight from the pool with her wet head and team sweats, sat stiffly on the floor. Lance, Cassidy and Eero were parked at the kitchen island sporting their own variations of poker faces. None of them looked directly at me. Not even sure anyone was breathing except of course Tillie the professional, who leveled her gazed at me lukewarmly from the kitchen table.

And then of course, there was Mitch.

He sat in the recliner, in jeans and a white hoodie, manspreading with his ankle resting on his knee. A folder on his lap had my name on it. Not a Dunes one, but official looking nonetheless.

I chuckled. Not that this scene itself was funny, but rather hilarious that I didn't see it coming. "So what the fuck is this? Group therapy? A roast?"

"What do you think it is, Nat?" Staci asked.

Again, I surveyed the room. Steeled expressions and stoic postures, like I was facing a firing squad. I squared my shoulders to engage and leveled my gaze at Mitch. "And why are you here? This isn't your business."

Our eyes met. Nothing, not a hint of emotion to read. He just sat there. Stone cold. A consummate professional.

"Mitch is here for the same reason everyone else is," Tillie said. "We're concerned."

"I bet you are," I replied, my sights still set on him. "You have a folder on me? Really? What did you psychoanalyze every fucking thing I ever said to you in confidence? Talk about betrayal."

"Natalie, he's not like that. You know that," Ari said.

"I have no idea who he is. Not anymore anyway."

Nothing registered on Mitch's face but I noticed his skin flush near his collar. Good. Shrinks like him were trained not to let crazy people like me rattle their cage, but maybe I still could. Call it payback for when he wasn't interested at all. "How dare you swoop in now? What for? Pity? Make yourself a hero?"

I glanced at Eero, who was clearly trying to read between the lines. He only knew Mitch in passing, had no idea there was a history between us. This wasn't how I wanted him to find out. Then again, I'd never planned for him to.

"Honey, all of us are here because we're worried about you," Tillie soothed. "Forget the clinical stuff. Just talk to us like your friends."

Cassidy slipped up beside me and wrapped her hand around my wrist. "Please, Nat. Just talk with us." She led me like I was radioactive to the other recliner facing the rest of the room, but I didn't take it. The competitor in me would never give up the edge of yielding to their wishes. So, I sank to the floor and folded my legs like a pretzel.

"I promise. No one's here to attack you," Tillie continued gently. "But everyone is a little concerned about what's going on with you lately and with what happened on the beach last night."

"Nothing happened last night," I told them. "I wasn't feeling well, so I went to bed. End of story."

"You're scaring people, Natalie," Ari said.

I rolled my eyes. "I am not. You're just being dramatic."

"You scared me," Cassidy added quietly.

"Well, if I did, I didn't mean to," I replied honestly.

Cassidy backed slowly to the couch and curled up like a kitten next to Ari, who put an arm around her. Upsetting Cassidy was the last thing I wanted to do. Her moods were so dependent on mine and her emotional capacity was always a question. So, I cleared my throat and mustered the widest smile I could.

"Cass, how about you grab one of those peach desserts Lance made for last night and eat it outside. It's a nice morning and I thought I saw a boat out there like the one on Bachelor in Paradise. You should check it out."

Cassidy sat up wide eyed. "Is there?"

We all watched her grab her treat from the fridge and head

out the sliding glass door. "Stay where we can see you from the window, please!" I called after her then addressed the rest of the room. "She doesn't need to be in here for this."

No one disagreed. No one spoke at all. I relented and sat down in the recliner and tucked my legs under myself. "Okay so let me have it!" I said with my hands outspread. "Bring it on. Tell me how worried you are and how my actions are affecting not just me but all of you. How put out you are by my behavior."

"You've been through something horrific," Tillie said simply. "It's catching up with you and we want to help. That's all."

I laughed. "Oh please, I'm not special. Who in this room hasn't been through something horrific?" My eyes fell on Eero and I realized maybe not *everyone*. "I'm fine. I just need to get my ass in shape, keep my head down, and focus."

"This isn't a swim race, Nat," Staci said. "And don't think we haven't put this all together."

"Put what together?"

"Seriously?" Staci asked, sharing a look with Lance. "We live with you. You think we don't notice when you don't go to class? You think we don't hear you at all hours of the night, walking around the house, or see that you eat like a gerbil? And you wear those long sleeves all the time because you've rubbed your wrists raw from those nervous ticks."

"Nervous ticks?" I snapped. "What am I, a tweaker now? My skin itches from all the chlorine I swim in every day."

"That's definitely not Swim Rash," Janessa said softly. "And the Pepperdine pool is brominated."

This felt like a very deep and dark corner I was being backed into. I swung my feet to the floor. "I'm not using. I swear to God, I haven't relapsed!"

"This isn't about drugs," Tillie blurted. "It's about Racer."

She said his name like she'd thrown down a gauntlet and the room froze. Even Mitch shifted, rubbing a hand over his face. I stared at the floor, at the veins in my feet, the chipped pink polish Ari had painted last week. I couldn't look up at them. If I did, I'd cry. Or scream. Or both.

"You don't have to go through this alone," Staci said. "You never did. We just didn't know how everything had snowballed until last night. I mean, school, swimming, Annie's foundation and now taking on the Marradine stuff. Maybe that's what triggered all of this. The Damian Cross case."

"I think there's something else that might be weighing on you, Natalie."

All eyes, including mine, landed on Mitch. He shifted in his seat, rolling his ballpoint pen thoughtfully between his fingers.

"Oh yeah?" I asked, as if accepting his challenge. "And what exactly is that?"

A silence opened up like a crater in the room. His gaze locked on mine and for a split second I was genuinely terrified at what he might reveal to this crowd of people.

"I've been in contact with the woman from the DA's office in Buffalo. The one coordinating victim impact statements for Racer's sentencing."

I looked up slowly. "You what?"

Mitch leaned forward with his elbows on his knees and his palms pressed together. His expression was all professional. Calm, like I was a wild animal he was afraid to spook. "When you didn't answer her calls or emails, I spoke to her myself. She wanted to know if I thought you'd be willing to speak. I told her I'd talk to you. I didn't promise anything, just that I'd check in."

"That's not your job," I said with a snarl.

"You're right, it's not. But I do know you. And I think it might help you to speak up and get things out in the open so you can really deal with them."

"Why the hell would I ever do that?"

He scanned the room before he refocused on me. This time with a softer expression, like we were the only two people in the space. "Because if you don't," he said, as if sharing a secret, "what Racer did to you could ruin every personal or intimate relationship you attempt for the rest of your life. That's not what you want, Natalie. And you know I know that."

The way he stared at me, his red-rimmed eyes hooded with concern, told me he was being sincere. Of course, I believed that before and I was clearly wrong then...

"Wow. I wish I'd realized sooner just how horrifyingly repulsive you find me. Was that it? You bust open my head, took a peek inside, and decided I was too broken to bother with? Just a mess you got tired of scraping off the floor."

"Jesus Christ, Natalie..." Mitch mumbled.

"What are you doing here anyway?" My voice cracked like a whip in the middle of the room. "How does this even concern you?"

Eero pushed off the kitchen wall. "He's here because he's a guy who knows what he's talking about," he snapped. "Because he's a professional who clearly cares about you. Like Tillie. He's trying to help."

"Help?" I laughed, bitter and hollow. "Are you the one who dragged everyone here? You think this confrontation is helping?"

"You think this is easy for me?" Eero's voice rose, something rare and raw. "You think any of this is fun for me? Watching you fall apart and not knowing how to reach you? Dealing with this...sex stuff?"

There it was.

He said it like it was a nuisance. Like I was some cold fish he was tired of angling. "Sex stuff?" I repeated, the tremble in my voice embarrassingly obvious. "I'm sorry me and my 'sex stuff' are such a disappointment."

"That's not what I said!"

"So, tell me the truth! Are you bored? Am I not putting out enough to keep you interested?"

"I don't mean it that way, Natalie!"

"Sorry I'm not the easy fuck you expected or what the whole world thinks I am! Go find Paris. She seems super accessible."

Everyone was stunned silent. I stood now in the middle of all of them, panting like the wind had been knocked out of me. Ari's hand covered her mouth as if she'd just watched a car crash. Janessa closed her eyes. Eero looked like I'd slapped him. Mitch stared at the floor, his hands fisted in his lap.

I blinked; my cheeks were suddenly wet. My lower lip trembled.

Tillie cleared her throat, calm but firm. "Natalie, I think you should go to Buffalo. To the impact hearing."

I laughed under my breath. "I can't just drop everything and fly across the country. You all just said I have a ton of things to handle here. Late start classes begin next week."

"You're not enrolled," Janessa said simply.

I turned, confused. "What?"

"You aren't allowed to register," she said, eyes steady. "You failed out. You couldn't go even if you wanted to?"

My mouth opened. Closed. My brain scrambled to deny it, but nothing came out.

"Then it's perfect!" Cassidy burst into the room with the wide smile of an eavesdropping eight-year-old who solved all the world's problems with a sugar fix. "You should go to Buffalo with Mitch. That's one of his jobs, right? Supporting people at stressful things so they don't lose their minds? He went with you last time to Annie's funeral."

Eero was standing by the window now, looking out. Arms crossed, his jaw tense. "I'm sorry, Natalie. I want to be supportive, but I don't get it. Not all of it and I don't know if I ever will." He turned toward me then, not angry, not pitying, just spent. "I don't know what it feels like to carry what you're carrying, and I'm not gonna pretend I do. I want to but...maybe I'm just standing in the way..."

The silence that followed was louder than anything anyone had said yet.

He looked at Mitch. "You're a professional, right? You know how to do this? How to be what she needs."

Mitch's eyes flicked to mine before he cleared his throat. "I'm not..." He shook his head before addressing Eero. "Look man, that's not how this works. This isn't something you just fix."

"If going to Buffalo helps her heal," Eero said, his voice catching, "then go. Be there. Whatever it takes. Just...just don't let her go through it alone."

Everyone glanced at everyone else looking for someone to protest. Mercifully, Tillie clapped her hands and folded them on the table. "Okay then, Natalie, do you agree that maybe this hearing is something you should do? If Mitch agrees to go with you for support, would that work?"

I swallowed hard. What choice did I have? They'd called out my every reason not to. It would just waste energy to fight it. "Fine," I said, barely louder than a whisper. "If this is what everyone thinks is best, I'll go."

Mitch nodded. Not in triumph or relief, just acknowledgment. Like this was happening, and there was no changing it now. "I'll make the arrangements," he said quietly. "The hearing is Monday. We can fly out tomorrow."

The words hit like a final stamp on something I hadn't even agreed to. I sat down hard on the edge of the armchair. My arms hung limp at my sides. I felt hollowed out. Like everything within me had been pulled out for display. A hand slipped over my shoulder. I looked up and there was Eero offering a sad smile. "I hope he helps you," he said, his voice rough. "Some of us don't come with degrees. Doesn't mean we weren't trying."

"Eero wait..."

But he was already walking toward the door. Not storming. Just done.

I wondered if we were, too.

———

The plane was quiet. That kind of heavy hush unique to red-eye flights when cabin lights dimmed and everyone's resigned themselves to the journey. I hadn't said much since takeoff and Mitch hadn't pushed. So, we just sat there, side by side, him in the window seat, me on the aisle. The space between us feeling like a rigid border neither of us dared to cross.

I thought about my big bon voyage back at the beach house. Tears and hugs. Tillie's final peptalk and Cassidy reminding me to watch The Bachelor on Monday night if I was still in Buffalo. Staci helped me pack sensible outfit choices. A lot of beige. Shoes without laces. Ari even pulled together a bag of makeup for me. All my best colors, winter tones (whatever that meant) she insisted. Makeup was the least of my priorities. I hadn't even worn lip gloss in months.

I still hated flying. The eerie groan of the engines. The smell of stale air and ammonia. Mitch on the other hand, seemed to rather enjoy it. Or at least was used to it. He leaned his head back, eyes just about closed. Like other than the human disaster sitting next to him, he didn't have a problem in the world.

For a split second, I let myself pretend it was months ago, back when we were still us. Maybe I'd lean in, brush against him like a cautious cat and he'd take the hint and wrap an arm around me. He'd hold me to his chest, and I'd listen to his steady heartbeat. Try to match my breathing to his, a weird thing I liked to do that never failed to sooth me.

"The nice thing about red-eye flights are the sunsets," Mitch said with his gaze now fixed out the window. "All the colors. All the quiet."

I rolled towards him. The golden light illuminated his face. The first time I saw him I thought he was gorgeous, any woman would with the short wavy blond hair and the cheek bones, and all the things Calvin Klein ads were known for. But he was also smart and kind and honest and strong. Everything that made us so wrong for each other.

"You know," he said finally, glancing over at me, "this is kind of familiar."

"How so?"

"When I brought you out here from Buffalo the first time. All strung out." He shook his head and smiled. "I'll never forget the look in your eyes. You were so pissed."

"Of course I was. I thought you were kidnapping me."

"You threatened to fake a seizure."

I cracked a reluctant smile. "You told me that wouldn't work because you were CPR certified."

"And you said, 'Guess we'll find out, won't we?'" He laughed, his eyes crinkling. "You were impossible, Collins."

"Still am," I said, but there wasn't any bite behind it.

He looked at me for a moment like he was considering a response, before he reached for his backpack and pulled out a slim, spiral-bound notebook. "I brought this for you," he said, placing it on the tray table in front of me. "Thought maybe you'd want to write something down. Like you used to."

"To whom, Annie?"

He shrugged. "Anyone you want. Marradine, Staci," he drew a breath and exhaled. "Eero."

I stared at it. The same kind of notebook Mitch gave to me years ago on our first flight together. I wrote endless letters to Annie, and even though I wasn't the recipient, they reminded me about what was important in my life.

"You remember that?" I asked softly.

"Of course I do."

I picked up the notebook, ran my fingers over the cover. "I haven't written to her since she died."

Mitch didn't say anything.

"Why are you here?" I asked him, not looking up. "I mean, really?"

He was quiet for a long time. "Because it's you. I know it's complicated. I mean, I met you through the Dunes but it's not like you were ever really a patient of mine. And now I'm just this guy who shows up when you need someone."

I laughed. "You mean like my keeper?"

He scoffed and looked me straight in the eyes. "No one keeps you, Natalie Collins. And that better not be what you're looking for."

"I'm just looking for some peace," I said honestly.

"I know." He slipped his hand over mine. "Maybe this trip will help the both of us."

"What do you mean? How would it help you?"

He lay his head back and closed his eyes. It was almost dark now, but I could still see the wrinkles in his forehead like something was bothering him. "What I mean is that after this trip, maybe we can both let some things go."

His voice was steady. Honest. It didn't feel like a line or a plea. We were attached to others now. There were boundaries. He was with Holly, and I was with Eero. Well, maybe I still was. Eero had been radio silent since the big scene at the beach house the day before. He told Janessa he was giving me space but I hadn't asked for any. "Thanks for coming Mitch," I whispered. "I'm sure it was a pain for you to be here."

"I'm here because I want to be," he assured me and gave my fingers a squeeze.

I closed the notebook and held it tight in my lap. "Okay," I said. "Then let's go speak some truth."

FOURTEEN

The lobby outside the courtroom was packed. Men, women, children, law enforcement, press all stood around shoulder to shoulder under yellow, fluorescent lights. It smelled like wet wood and floor cleaner and gave off the vibe of Hell's Waiting Room. I shuddered at the thought of what loomed beyond those closed doors at the other end of the hall.

"Do you think they already started?" I looked up at Mitch standing like a sentinel beside me. He wore courtroom-respectable jeans and a white sweater he claimed was one of his sentimental favorites from his Idaho days. Despite his height, even he had to evaluate the dense crowd on the tiptoes of his Timberlands. "I'm not sure," he said taking my hand in his. "Come on, let's get you in there."

But just as we attempted to navigate the mob, the heavy wooden courtroom doors swung open. People emerged.

"Wait, is everyone leaving?" I asked.

A row of young girls hurriedly filed out and headed in our direction. Some stunned, almost catatonic while others were agitated and wild-eyed. One of them, about sixteen, looked at me as she passed. A tall brunette in a tasteful beige sweaterdress with her hair pulled neatly back in a bun. I realized I barely dragged a brush through my own mophead before I put it up, but at least it was washed. As were my jeans, my plain black long-sleeved t-shirt and the heavy black hoody I layered because I didn't own a winter coat anymore.

I gave Mitch's hand a tug. "The hearing's not over, is it?"

He pulled his phone from his back pocket and checked the time. "Nine-thirty, right? We should be right on time."

The crowd followed as the girls kept marching past us like a small, battle-weary army. There had to be thirty of them. Tall, short, brunette, blonde, big, small, dressed in everything from dresses to torn jeans all walking with their heads down and shoulders hunched. Makeup ran down their cheeks and the red circles rimmed their eyes.

"No," I whispered and started to push down the hall in the direction they came from. "No," I said again, louder this time. "We missed it?"

Mitch caught up to me. "Natalie..."

"It went quicker than they planned." An older woman with a stack of folders came up to us, lifting her cheaters to the top of her grey head. "You never know with these things. Sometimes it takes days. Sometimes, the survivors just don't have the stomach to say much. Especially when a scum bag like this guy doesn't have any remorse." She turned to look at me. "I assume you're one of them?"

I felt Mitch slip a large hand over my shoulder. "Yeah, I'm one of them."

"I'm sorry," the woman said.

Before I could say anything else, a tall man in a suit came rushing at me down the hall. He thrust his pointer finger at me. "Hey! That's Natalie Collins!"

My stomach dropped.

And suddenly, a fresh deluge of people materialized as if from nowhere. Some with TV cameras, most with recording phones circled around me. I backed myself up against the wall preparing for the onslaught.

"Natalie! Why weren't you in the courtroom today?"

"Do you have anything to say about the hearing?"

"Are you planning to make your impact statement privately?"

"What would you say to Racer Jameson if you had the chance?"

That one landed like a slap. I froze, every part of me locking up at once. Flashes popped. Microphones were shoved in my face. I saw the red light blinking on a camera just over someone's shoulder. A live feed.

My mouth opened, but nothing came out. I couldn't speak. I couldn't think. All I could see in my mind's eye were the faces of the girls I'd passed in the hallway, every one of them trying to hold themselves together the same way I was now, unsuccessfully.

"She isn't making a statement to you guys," Mitch said sharply, stepping between me and the wall of reporters. "Give her space. Back off."

But they didn't. The questions kept coming.

"Natalie, do you blame the DA for the scheduling error?"

"Do you plan on using your notoriety to advocate against sexual abuse?"

I was limp. Incredulous. In California, this all seemed controllable. Out of sight out of mind, until the memories found me and consumed me. If living my reality was bad enough out west, being back in Buffalo, the proverbial scene of the fucking crime, it was much worse. "I gotta get out of here," I said to no one. Anyone. "I just...I can't."

"Come on," Mitch said.

Like thieves making a getaway, he yanked me through the crowd and around the corner, using his football assets of size and agility to maneuver. Finally, we made it through the lobby, into the stairwell and took the two flights down to street level. We stopped at the bottom to catch our breaths. I closed my eyes and lay my head back against the cool concrete, trying to will my heartbeat back to calm.

Mitch rested his hands on his hips and gave me a once-over. "You okay?" he asked, though his tone made it clear he already knew the answer.

"No," I said honestly. "Not even close."

"I'm sorry," he ran his hand through his hair and paced the landing in frustration. "I should've double-checked the time. I should've gotten us here earlier."

"Don't do that. Don't make this about a clock."

He stopped in his tracks and glared at me. It wasn't often I could call him out of *his* bullshit.

"So, what do we do now?" I asked, more to the universe than to either of us standing there. "I came all this fucking way for nothing."

"No, you didn't." Mitch came toward me, wrapping his hands over my shoulders. "Listen to me. You faced it, Natalie. You did what you needed to do."

"But I didn't say anything!" I screamed, angrily shrugging off his grip. "He never EVER gave me the chance to say a damn thing!"

"I know," he said softly.

"No, you sure as hell don't know, Mitch! He didn't drug you and whore you out to all his damn friends while you just lay there and took it!"

"No, you're right, he didn't," he said even softer.

"I wish you could understand! I wish you could just see for a minute how it consumes my mind! How I think about if I could have just said 'no' to him, or any of his disgusting friends one motherfucking time, he wouldn't have ruined almost everything in my life! My career! My family! Us..."

Mitch cocked his chin like he was deflecting a blow. I could tell he was trying really hard to keep his own shit together but the glaze in his eyes told me he was failing.

I sniffled and wiped a tear from my eye. "Don't you see how helpless I feel...?"

"Christ Natalie, of course I see it! I'm trained to fucking see it!"

I nearly jumped from my skin when his voice boomed like thunder off every wall in the stairwell. He came towards me as if possessed, red-faced and tense with an uncontrolled anger I'd never seen from him before. "You think watching you go through this, scared and confused, doesn't tear me up inside? You think it doesn't kill me knowing I can't reach you? That you're terrified of my touch? That you can't trust me with your body? You think I don't hate him for that? Do you think that because I have some kind of psychological insight into this stuff this hasn't broken my heart?"

"Mitch, please don't..."

"Do you have any idea about how I feel about you? How I feel about all of this?"

Down the hall a buzzer sounded alerting us to an open door and people walking out to the street. Dazed, we watched through the window as a Buffalo Police transport van pulled up to the curb. Two officers stepped out. Two more walked a prisoner toward them.

Between them, handcuffed, was Racer.

I froze stone cold.

This. This was the moment I was waiting for.

Like something inhuman propelled me, I burst out the door to the sidewalk. I jumped into his path...

And there we were, face to repulsive face. The image I was too sick, sad, and scared to fully realize in my nightmares, was right in front of me now. He weirdly looked younger than I remembered. His long stringy hair was buzzed and he was clean shaved. He looked pale. Stunned. Like I'd forced him into an unwanted engagement.

How'd that feel asshole?

I stepped closer until the officer beside him raised a hand. "Ma'am—"

"It's okay," I said. "I just need one second."

Racer didn't speak. He didn't blink. I didn't expect him to.

I stepped forward, leaned in...

"Look I know you don't give a shit about me or the rest of those girls in there so whether I say my piece to you or to everyone in that courtroom or to the Channel Seven Eyewitness News, it doesn't matter. I just need to say it out loud and get rid of this poison inside of me.

"You are a monster. A disgusting predator who took everything from me. I was a girl with problems and pressures, and you saw those things as fucking opportunity. You victimized and abused and used me however you fucking wanted to, and you did it over and over and over again!"

"Miss, we have to take the prisoner now..."

"Fuck you!" I glared at the guard then at Mitch who stood beside me with a steel in his eyes. I took it in and turned back to Racer.

"Did it make you feel good? Did it make you and all your friends feel strong? To steal my voice, to violate me in every possible way your demonic mind could conjure?"

"Seriously Miss, we have to go."

"Wait!" Again, I stepped forward daring myself to look in his eyes. The dark murky brown ones that bound me in my sleep. It was mine who held his now. I was in control. This wasn't a dream but a reality of my choosing.

This was my last motherfucking chance.

"I'm done letting you make my decisions. I'm done with you driving people I love away. I'm done letting you ruin my life. I'm choosing my own life now."

What happened immediately after that I don't remember. Just that I took a step back, breathing in the cold air. It felt sharp, clean, and energizing. Not the way one would usually describe the atmosphere of an inner-city Buffalo back alley. One of the guards gave me a quick, respectful nod before pulling Racer away. Racer didn't look back.

Mitch stepped beside me. Not touching, not moving. Just there.

"Oh my God," I mumbled because I didn't know what else to say.

"Well, that fucking happened," he said after a moment. His voice was soft, but I heard the thread of pride in it. "You didn't need a courtroom for that scene to count."

I gave a half-laugh, half-exhale. "I thought I was gonna pass out."

"But you didn't."

"I might still."

He smiled a little. "Then let's find somewhere with heat and caffeine before that happens."

We turned away from the transport van together, walking into the bright white light of the Buffalo morning. My legs were still shaky, but my spine? Straight as hell.

Where to next?

———

We spent the day doing mindless winter things in Western New York. The stuff Rom Com movie montages were made of. Spicy Buffalo Wings plates for lunch, ice skating on Lake Erie in the afternoon, a Sabers hockey game at night. There was a point along the way, I think over hot chocolate at Dell's Café, that I realized I'd mastered the art of compartmentalizing myself. There was Chill Natalie who loved junk food, snowy days, and pretending everything was fine. While Deeply Traumatized Natalie just crossed her fingers and prayed that someday, somehow, Chill Natalie might actually help Trauma Natalie get her shit together.

Both incarnations missed Mitch desperately.

It was past eleven when I stepped out of the hotel shower. It was steamy and smelled like a nostalgic mixture of Mitch's musky body wash, and the strawberry lotion I'd just slathered on. SportsCenter hummed low from the other room, his usual sleep soundtrack. It felt good to know I still remembered his habits.

I pulled on flannel pajama pants and a baggy white tee, letting my hair down from a clip. It had been a decent day, but I knew better than to assume the night would follow. If I managed to fall asleep without lavender or anything else from my bag of tricks, I'd call it a win.

I turned off the light and stepped out of the bathroom. The room was dark, save for the amber glow of a streetlamp leaking through the curtains and the glare of the television. I padded over to my bed but just stood there, aware of Mitch in the other. I could hear his deep breaths. Even and steady. I thought about all that transpired in the past twelve hours. The courtroom, the sidewalk confrontation, and everything after that filled the space and busied our minds. Suddenly the separation felt wrong and sad. Like if I slept alone, the distance would be more terrifying than the closeness.

So, I turned and slipped in beside him.

The sheets were cool, but I could feel his heat. The kind that made you melt and your eyelids flutter. I lay on my side to face him. I'd done this before. Look him over. Study him. Try to memorize the line of his jaw and the curve of his muscles. He was on his back, shirtless, the edge of the comforter resting just below his ribs. The football player/military man physique he spent a ton of time in the gym to maintain was enhanced by the permanent tan I'd always known him to have. He had the softest skin and it always amused me that for a man so rigidly cut under it, there was no softer place to land than in his arms. I remembered that. There was so much I remembered, in fact.

But some things I wished I'd forget...

It was months ago. A Sunday night, just before Mitch was leaving for Marine training in San Diego. A Bills game had gone into overtime, and we watched over steaks and cheesecake. We were tangled up on his couch, kissing like we knew we'd be apart for a while.

Like this would finally be 'the night.'

We'd been in this position before, these escalated, middle-school-caliber make-out sessions because sometimes my desire won out over my anxiety. There were occasions when I was okay with even more. Where I'd clumsily undress him and explore his body with open palms and he'd watch me do so with lustful eyes. Tell me in strained whispers how beautiful and special I was in between gentle kisses. I believed him. I believed in him. He wouldn't lie or betray me. I trusted him more than I trusted myself.

I remembered him looming over me as I settled myself back on the couch. He was shirtless, his face flushed with whips of his short blond hair damp at his forehead. He smiled sweetly but there was raw desire in his eyes. We both wanted this and I recalled in that moment I felt grateful, fucking relieved that maybe, just maybe, I could still relate to a man the way a woman was supposed to. Like all the things I had held inside me that Racer stole hadn't hollowed me out completely.

But somewhere between Mitch lowering himself to me, the kisses he trailed down my neck and the anticipation of feeling him inside of me, something heavy and sinister came over me. What if I wasn't capable of giving him everything he deserved? What if that was where it ended for me? For us?

The panic had come hard and fast. Like a woman possessed, I yanked off my t-shirt and bra and pulled him back on top of me. I kissed him forcefully, desperately, sloppily. I babbled about how I needed him, wanted him, anything that might have convinced him, convinced *me* that I was fine. I wasn't.

I unzipped his jeans and began to stroke him. He was so hard but I could tell by the way he trembled he was holding himself back. I held him tight, perversely proud that I could fake my way through this as long as he was satisfied. I unzipped my own jeans. If I could just get it over with...

"Natalie, wait..."

His lips tightened, then broke away from mine as he eased my hand from his pants.

"What...?" I stammered. "Why...?"

"It can't happen this way. This isn't right."

I remember jerking myself up from under him, burning with the shame I thought I deserved. He reached for me but I pushed him away and then I laughed it off like it was some sort of misguided game. I teased him about Bills fans being allergic to intimacy. About how I figured eight weeks in Marine training earned him one for the road. Anything to patch over the crack that I had inadvertently just opened up between us.

I couldn't.

Later that night when he fell asleep, I slipped out the door. He left for boot camp the next morning and I'd ignored him the best I could ever since. He had been unreachable in San Diego anyway, but when he came back, dodging him took effort. Staci and the gang would invite him to get-togethers at the beach house or I'd see him in passing at the Dunes, but I'd avoid him. Clearly my MO for a lot of things. Soon he got the picture. And now he was with Holly.

Good for him.

A car horn from the hotel parking lot below pulled me from my thoughts. My fingertips now rested lightly on Mitch's arm, tracing a fading scar near his elbow that was new since I'd last been in a position like this. He turned his head and blinked at me, his eyes heavy with sleep. He didn't flinch. Didn't move away.

His voice came out low, rough, intimate. "Hey, you good?"

"I think so. Maybe I'll finally get some sleep tonight."

Mitch's hand found mine under the covers, his fingers brushing lightly over my knuckles. Comfort. Reassurance. "I'm proud of you, Nat," he said. "For today. For showing up. For saying what needed to be said."

The lump in my throat rose so fast I almost couldn't breathe around it. "Thank you, for making me come out here."

Mitch exhaled, a sound almost like a laugh. "I'm sorry for that ambush intervention scene back at the house. It wasn't exactly protocol, but we were all just scared."

"You know you're officially banned from my Dunes provider list now, right?"

Again, he laughed. "Yeah, fair. Probably not the cleanest display of therapeutic ethics."

"It's okay. I'm glad you overstepped."

He closed his eyes and shook his head. "I've been so damn worried about you, Nat. You have no idea. Those eight weeks I was in San Diego you were all I thought about."

"I was just doing some thinking myself. About that night at your place."

I felt him stiffen against me so I scootched over to him even closer, my stomach pressed to his hip and my leg over his.

"I thought you didn't want me," I said, my voice barely above a whisper. "I thought that maybe I turned you off somehow."

"Natalie, that's not at all how I felt, believe me." He reached up, slow and careful, to tuck a piece of hair behind my ear. "I wanted you," he said. "God, Natalie. Of course, I wanted you. I just recognized your mood for what it was. You needed to feel normal and were trying to prove something."

God was he good. So annoyingly in tune to the misfires in my head. "Consequences for being with a therapist," I teased.

"I never wanted to be your therapist," he corrected. "I just wanted to be the man that did right by you. I still do."

"I still want you to be."

That truth felt fragile and huge all at once. I closed my eyes, pressing my forehead into the space between his jaw and shoulder and wrapping my arm around him. He pulled me close, practically on top of him. We stayed like that for a long time.

"I haven't..." I started, then faltered. I pulled back just enough to look at him.

"You asked me before if I slept with Eero."

Mitch's face didn't change much. "I know," he said softly.

"You do?" I asked, feeling suddenly stupid, exposed.

He gave the smallest nod. "Well, maybe I just don't want to know any different. I don't want to think about you and any other man in a position to hurt you. You know what it took to not level that asshole in the alley today? I've been wanting to kill him for three years."

"I'm not sure I even know *how* to want that anymore," I said.

"You just need some more time," he soothed, mindlessly running his fingers up and down my back like he was calming the both of us.

"And then there's you and Holly," I said, half-statement, half-question.

"Yeah. Holly and I." He exhaled through his nose, like even saying it out loud didn't sit quite right. "I don't know how serious it is," he admitted. "She's figuring herself out. We both are."

"She knows about us?" I asked.

"Parts," he said. "Enough to know you matter."

I was quiet for a long moment. Finally, I summoned the courage to ask. "What's it like with her? I mean, the sex."

He shifted under me, like the strange question surprised him. "Well, I guess it's just comfortable," he admitted. "Mutual. No expectations. No deep stuff. Sometimes funny, honestly. She talks a lot."

That made me smile. "Of course she does."

"It's not fireworks but it's not bad either. It's something in between."

I sat with that a moment, watching my finger trace a line over one of his ab muscles. "Did you ever wonder what it would've been like with us?"

"All the time," he said. No hesitation.

"What did you think our first time would be like?"

He slid out from beneath me to where I was under him now. He looked me in the eyes. Like he'd been wanting and waiting for me to ask him this very question.

"Slow," he said tenderly his hand sliding down the exposed skin of my arm. "Intense. I'd try to give you exactly what you needed...what you desired." He leaned in, his eyes closing, his breath warm near my temple. "Every kiss, every touch, we'd both feel it. What's between us." His lips brushed my cheek then drifted to my ear. "I'd make love to you, Natalie. Simple as that."

My hand rested on his chest, directly over his hammering heart. He caressed the nape of my neck, holding me there, like maybe he wanted something more but was waiting for me to move first.

So I did.

I tilted my face up toward his. Slowly, cautiously. His eyes met mine in the dark, searching as if afraid to hope. Our lips touched, a kiss, so soft it barely existed. Not hungry. Not carnal. Just real.

When we finally parted, our foreheads rested together, breaths mingling, hearts loud in the quiet. His thumb grazed my cheekbone like I might shatter. "Please don't tell me that was a mistake," I whispered. "Because it wasn't."

"No," he murmured, his lips moving once more against mine. "We would never be a mistake. I just need you to know what I feel for you...it never left."

I shifted closer, rolling and curling against him like a small spoon. His arms came around me instantly, instinctively, like I belonged there.

"I think when we get back to California, I'm just going to focus on the auction," I said seemingly out of nowhere. "On the foundation. I just want to be useful to someone."

"You think that'll help?"

I nodded against his chest. "Helping others is the only thing that's ever helped me. It's how I survived with Annie. It's how I'll keep surviving now."

He pressed a kiss onto the top of my head. "You're okay," he whispered. "You're safe and exactly where you're supposed to be."

We didn't say anything else.

We didn't need to.

FIFTEEN

Dear Mrs. Harriman
February 5, 11:46 a.m.

I'm so sorry I missed the hearing yesterday. The truth is,
I was there. I made the trip all the way from Los Angeles to
Buffalo, and somehow, I missed it by a few minutes. Please
know I'm deeply sorry for being so difficult over these past
few months. It wasn't because I didn't care. It was because
the idea of giving a victim impact statement felt like admitting there was closure, that I had something neat and final to
say about what Racer did to me.

You see, I'm still figuring it out.

I'm trying damn hard to move forward, to live my life in
a way that's healthy, honest, and real. To take back the parts
of myself he stole, the parts that know how to connect with
people, to trust, to love. I'm writing this from the plane
home, sitting beside a friend who understands how hard this
journey has been. And for the first time in a long time, I feel
something lighter.

Like I can finally stop hurting myself and start helping others again.

When I get back to Los Angeles, I'm hosting an art auction to raise money for kids and families facing cancer. It's the kind of work that reminds me who I am. Who I want to be. I don't have all the next steps figured out yet. School, career, the rest of my life. It all still feels wide open. Thank you for helping me realize it was time to stop standing still. I'm moving forward now.

Sincerely,

Natalie

———

THE NIGHT I GOT HOME, it was sunny and warm. A total shift from the frigid snowscape I'd just left behind. The gang gave me a choice between a beachside cookout and a grease-fest at The Barn. Despite the gorgeous weather, I went with our dark, familiar sports bar. I could tell they were dying for the tea about my trip, and honestly, I was way more likely to spill over a plate of nachos than under the open sky.

We crammed into the big round booth in the corner. Staci, Ari, Cassidy, Janessa, Lance, and me. The table was buried under every appetizer you could think of. Mozzarella sticks, chicken wings, chips, salsa, and a sad little tray of veggies no one was touching. Cassidy was already halfway through a Shirley Temple, stabbing cherries with her straw and sneaking glances at an episode of *The Voice* playing, ironically, on mute.

"Sooo," Ari said, leaning forward and venturing carefully with the straw of her Diet Coke on her lips. "No Eero tonight, huh?"

I shrugged, trying to keep my voice casual. "I called him.

Texted, too. I know he had a meet earlier, but I figured he'd at least hit me back."

Staci raised an eyebrow. "You think he's bent out of shape because you went to Buffalo with Mitch?"

"It's not like I went on vacation with him," I said quickly. "It was complicated. And short. Mitch was just there for moral support."

Janessa gave me a look. "But you know how that sounds to a guy, right? Some other dude takes her away..."

I groaned. "You all know that it was so not like that."

Cassidy leaned forward, chin in her hand. "Do you think Eero thinks it was?"

I hesitated. "I don't know. I think Eero's trying to understand what I'm going through, but I don't think he really does. And Mitch being around probably makes it worse."

Staci gave a small nod, chewing on a mozzarella stick. "Guys always say they're chill until they're not."

"I just don't want to feel like I have to manage everyone's emotions on top of my own," I admitted.

"You don't," Ari said, reaching across to squeeze my wrist. "We're just glad you're home."

I told them about missing the hearing, about Racer's face, about the reporters and the cameras and the panic. I didn't gloss over it. I didn't have to. They just nodded like they were proud. Like they'd been waiting for me to get my head straight. Or at least, straighter.

"I know I gave you all hell about going," I said, setting my glass down. My voice wobbled a little, but I didn't try to hide it. "But thanks for getting in my face about it. Maybe that's what I needed."

"Have you thought about what the next steps are?" Ari asked as she dragged a mozzarella stick through the puddle of ranch dressing on her plate. "I mean, I know you just got home, and I know this has been weighing on your mind."

"As far as school, the semester is started so I can't do much there."

"Maybe start planning for the fall," Janessa suggested. "Registration is right around spring break. As long as you deal with the academic hold, you can pick your classes."

"If I knew what I was taking," I picked a chip off my plate and popped it in my mouth. "I'm not even sure when I was in class if I was there for the right reasons. More to distract my mind than to learn anything."

"Have you thought about swimming?" Janessa asked.

"Yeah, I was thinking about that on the flight home. Swimming is the one thing I really miss. But I'm not sure if it's because I miss Annie or the actual sport."

"So, you're saying you want to get back in the pool?" Staci asked.

"I'm saying I want to feel good about myself, and when I think about all the times that I was truly happy in my own skin, I was in the pool. I don't know if that makes it a right choice, but it makes it better than where I am now."

"But you have to be an enrolled student to be on the team," Janessa said. "I mean I know you're Natalie Collins international swimmer extraordinaire, but I don't think even Coach Matthews is allowed to let you into the pool unless you're part of the University."

"You could try to be in the Olympics again."

We all looked at Cassidy hyper-focused on her placemat she was coloring with a red Crayon. "If you like coach Matthews so much and you're still really good at swimming, why not try again to be the best at something you love? That seems like the most positive thing you could do."

"She kind of has a point," Lance said.

Cassidy beamed and immediately knocked over her Shirley Temple, sending pink liquid across the table. Lance swore and jumped up to grab napkins while Cassidy frantically tried to mop it up with the end of her sleeve. "Oops."

"Classic Collins chaos," Lance said, grinning at me. "Who wants to play some darts?"

"I'm in," Ari said. Janessa got up from the table with her.

"Great," Staci said. "How about Cassidy and Lance against Ari and Janessa. Nat and I get winners."

We watched the crew weave through the patrons to the back dartboard. Staci looked me over playing with the straw of her root beer. "They'll be gone a while. Why don't you fill me in an all the below the surface stuff." Her mouth twitched. "So did you and Mitch smooth things over?"

I sighed, smiling a little. "It's just being around him. It's different. It's like he doesn't see the mess and the damage first. He sees me and he doesn't flinch."

Staci's face softened. "He always has, Nat."

I nodded.

"You shared a room, right?" Staci leaned in and lowered her voice. "Did anything happen, physically? I mean, I know considering the reason you were there that seems like a weird question..."

"There were separate beds," I said quickly.

"He was so worried about you," she said. "He tried to play it cool, but he wasn't. He really cares about you, Nat. Not because he feels sorry for you. Because he believes in you."

"I don't know if I deserve that," I whispered.

"Do you think if you got past some things the two of you could, maybe, be something?"

I pushed my plate aside and folded my arms on the table.

There was very little I would hold back from Staci. Since the Dunes, she was my best friend and sounding board in every way. Mitch was one of the very few topics where I kept some details to myself. Maybe I was romanticizing or just straight up embarrassed, but there had been moments between Mitch and me too deep to bring out to the light. Sacred. Even though we weren't together, I still felt that way.

"He's got enough to deal with anyway," I told her. "Holly. His new job. He doesn't have time to police my crazy."

"What about Eero?" Staci asked casually, almost too casually.

I shrugged. "He was at a swim meet this weekend. Some invitational thing. We texted a few times. Nothing deep. Just updates."

Staci nodded like she already knew. "Look, Eero is a nice guy, and from what I can see he's trying to understand. But he doesn't know how to reach you without fixing you. And you're not a problem to fix."

"It's not his fault," I said. "He's good. He just doesn't fit into this part of my story."

"Maybe not. Or maybe not yet. Either way, you're allowed to be honest about what you need."

The waiter dropped off a tower of garlic knots and the spell was broken. Staci grabbed a fresh napkin and put one on her plate. "Speaking of moving forward," she said, "you're about to have a hell of a project waiting for you."

I blinked. "The auction?"

She pulled out her phone and scrolled. "We've got about fifty pieces confirmed," she said. "Photographs, paintings, some sculptures. A few really big names too. Enough to make it a serious event." She showed me her screen.

"Wow," I breathed. "That's...that's a lot."

Staci smiled. "It's gonna be good, Nat. You're gonna be good." She tore a garlic knot in half and popped a piece into her mouth.

"I'll go to the gallery with you tomorrow, of course, but I also want to go see Marradine. There's some stuff I'd like to say to her. Even if she can't talk back, or doesn't want to."

"Bullseye!" Cassidy screamed with her hands in the air. "Suck it Ari and Janessa! I'm unstoppable!"

I laughed and gave her a thumbs up, inspired by her confidence. I was grabbing my own garlic knot when the door to the restaurant banged open behind us. Every head in the place swiveled toward the girl in dark sunglasses with an Idaho State football cap pulled down over her face.

Holly?

She was breathless, and anxious like she'd sprinted across the parking lot. Her beige blouse was wrinkled, one strap of her coordinating Coach bag sliding off her shoulder. She scanned the place like it wasn't where she meant to be.

"What the hell is she doing here?" Staci muttered under her breath. "She looks like she's on a mission."

"Shit," I murmured. "Do you think she's here to confront me? About Mitch? About Buffalo?"

"Nothing happened you said," Staci hissed. "You don't have anything to explain. Mitch would never violate your trust."

Holly spotted us and hurried over to the table, nearly knocking over a waitress and bumping a tray off a table along the way. "Natalie, please, please forgive me for just showing up, but I really need to talk to you."

"Um... Is everything all right?"

She hesitated, glancing at Staci. "I mean, not really," she wiped away a tear on her cheek. "That's why I'm here. I need to talk to you in private."

Holly, Staci, and I headed out to Staci's Wrangler. Not that it was much more private than inside the restaurant, but at least it was dark so it wouldn't be as obvious if a paparazzi was hanging around. Holly slid into the passenger side, I sat behind the wheel, and Staci was in the backseat. Engine off, lights out. Awkward.

"I came here on a hunch," Holly said, glancing out the windshield like she expected someone to jump out. "Lance invited Mitch and me tonight, but Mitch is working late, and I thought you'd be here. Your friends do Tuesday nights at this place, right?"

"Usually," I said slowly.

"That's really special to have such a big group of friends." She slipped off her sunglasses and looked down at her folded hands. The light baby pink nails almost glistened in the moonlight. "Must be nice. I just kind of hang out with my brother's friends."

"Are you okay?" I asked. "I mean, you said you had something to tell me."

"I didn't know what else to do," she admitted. "I didn't want Mitch to know I was coming here. I know he'd ask questions."

"About what?" I asked.

"Marradine," Holly whispered. "She asked to see me. While you two were in Buffalo."

I stiffened. "Why? What did she say?"

"She didn't *say* anything obviously." Holly looked around the car before leaning in closer and lowering her voice. "She kept asking what Karl Rollings gave you, what he said. And she asked about the paintings."

The weight of her words landed hard. "What about them?"

"She said she needs to be at the auction. That it matters. That something happened that night...and she thinks she remembers it now."

Staci and I exchanged a glance.

"I didn't understand at first," Holly went on. "But then she kept writing the same thing. Breath mints. Over and over. Like it meant something."

I blinked. "Breath mints?"

"She asked if I remembered seeing Karl Rollings that night. I told her I did. That I saw him leave the party at the main house and head down the path toward the stables. That didn't sit with me right and I told my brother about it, but he didn't seem to care so I told Damian. I think Damian confronted Karl."

My pulse spiked. "Why didn't you say anything sooner?"

"Because I didn't know it mattered!" Her voice cracked. "And then today, Marradine just...she looked terrified. She wouldn't stop writing. She kept asking if you got anything from Karl. If you talked to him."

Staci leaned back in her seat, exhaling slowly. "Jesus."

"I don't think she's safe and I got the impression she doesn't think you are either because she talks to you," Holly whispered. "I don't know what she remembers exactly, but it's clearly scary to her."

"Do you think she's ready to tell the truth?" I asked.

"I don't know," Holly said. "But I think she wants to. She wouldn't have asked me to come otherwise. And I think she wants you to help her."

We sat in silence, the reality pressing down like a storm front.

"She wants to go to the auction," Holly added. "She knows it's this weekend but she didn't know if she'd see you before then. She made me promise to tell you."

I met her eyes. "I planned on going to see her tomorrow."

We sat there for a moment. An agreement reached. Staci and I looked at each other, waiting for Holly to initiate a marginally graceful exit from the car. She didn't.

"You know I'm really sorry that happened to you," Holly blurted, nervously fidgeting with her new bracelet dangling from her wrist. "I mean with that Racer guy. I know I don't know you very well. I only know what Mitch tells me, and he thinks really highly of you. I can tell he's been worried about what's going on."

"Mitch is a really good guy," I said to her. "And it takes a lot for me to say that because trusting men doesn't come very easily to me anymore."

"I get it." She nodded. "Look, I'm not some Hollywood party girl. I'm just a corn-fed midwestern army brat whose brother happened to make it big. He's paying for my vet school."

"You're in vet school?"

"I start in the fall." She shrugged. "I befriended Marradine because I thought she could use one. She's famous and all, but clearly, she's really struggling."

"It's nice you still talk to her after she drove you through the front of Ralph Lauren."

We both laughed. The sound came quickly and disappeared just as fast.

Holly shifted, suddenly remembering herself. "I should go. Please don't tell Mitch I was here."

"I won't."

She slipped out of the car and disappeared into the parking lot. Staci and I just sat there. Stunned. "Well, that's not what I thought that convo would be about."

"Nope," I agreed. "Me either."

"What the hell did we get ourselves into?" Staci asked.

"No. Fucking. Idea."

We jumped at a sudden banging on the passenger window. Cassidy.

"Come on, you guys!" she shouted "Everyone's waiting! I won and now it's your turns to go down!"

Staci and I shared a look. Damn, I hoped she was wrong.

SIXTEEN

MARRADINE SAT cross-legged on the Dunes south lawn near the rosebushes I used to spend hours pruning with Tillie. It impressed me how much they'd grown in three years. Back then they were about my height, and they were skinny enough I could reach around their circumference, if I didn't mind an armful of thorns. Now I had to strain my neck and squint at the sun to see the tops of them.

The late afternoon light made the whole place glow soft and gold, like something out of a dream. Marradine had a sketchpad balanced on her knees. I'd decided I wasn't going to tell her I knew Holly had visited, or even that Marradine reached out to her in the first place. The thing was, I really was just a friendly ear to this girl whose position was weirdly close to mine three years earlier. I wasn't a detective. I wasn't even a true crime junkie. I was just trying to be a nice person.

I crossed the lawn slowly. Despite the hour, the heat still baked me in my black t-shirt and matching shorts. Heat made me claustrophobic from time to time so I pushed my sleeves up over my shoulders a la instant tank top style, like that would ever help. When I reached her, I sat down a few feet away on the grass, pulling my knees up to my chest. No hellos. No smiles. I wasn't even sure she knew I was there she was so still. So, I just started talking.

"Sorry I haven't been around," I said as more of a greeting than apology. "I meant to tell you I was leaving town for a few days, but the last time we hung out you got pretty pissed and I didn't have a chance to come back and tell you."

She reached into the pocket of her khaki shorts and pulled out a folded piece of paper, worn soft around the edges. She held it out to me without a word. I took it carefully, smoothing it open.

In her uneven handwriting...

Saw the news. Sorry you didn't get to speak. But I'm happy you went.

I blinked at it. Holly must have told her, had to have. The Dunes didn't exactly stream breaking headlines.

"Thanks," I said softly. "It helped. It sucked, but it helped."

We sat there for a long moment. I wasn't sure of the vibe. Was she mad at me still? Scared? Curious? All three?

"Look Marradine, I'm not here to pressure you," I said carefully. "But I want you to know I'm not stupid. I know something happened the night Damian died. Something you haven't said out loud yet."

She didn't react. No scribbled note. No flinch. But I knew she heard me.

"You reached out to Holly. You asked about Karl Rollings. The paintings. The breath mints. That wasn't random." I drew in a breath, the heat making it feel heavier than it was. "I'm not trying to out you. I'm not the cops. But if Damian or anyone hurt you, if someone took something from you, you deserve to take something back. Even if it's just the truth."

Still silence. But something in her face changed. Barely, but it was there. A flicker of recognition. Of fear.

"I'm having that art auction this weekend. Some of Damian's collection will be there. If it feels like something you need to see, or face, or confront, come. I'll take you myself. No one has to know unless you want them to."

She scribbled something quickly, tore the sheet off, and held it up.

The press would eat me alive.

"The press can go fuck themselves," I replied. "This is your call. I just want you to know...you won't be alone."

She finally gave me a nod. Small. But real. It was enough.

By the time I headed back across the grounds to the employee commissary, the sun had slipped behind the trees. I headed straight for the coffee bar, not even watching where I was going, too deep in my own thoughts when I nearly collided with someone.

Holly stood at the counter, pouring oat milk into a paper cup. Her pale-yellow blouse was rumpled, her chestnut hair barely holding together in a loose knot. She looked like she'd been pacing hallways all day. Probably had, tagging along with Mitch, waiting for this moment, hoping for a run-in.

"Did you talk to her?" she asked, not looking up.

"I did," I said. "Did you?"

She nodded. "Earlier. She didn't say anything but she looked scared. Shaky. She kept writing the same things over and over again, still asking about Karl Rollings, the paintings..."

"She remembers," I said quietly. "Not everything. But enough of it."

"I feel so bad for her. I should have told someone," Holly murmured.

"What do you mean?" I reached for my own paper cup and the coffee pot. "Told someone what?"

"She was always in that barn. Who knows what she was doing down there. Maybe that's where she kept her drugs."

I blinked at her, confused by the shift in conversation. "Holly, I don't think this is about drugs. This is about these guys, your brother included by the way, who were all down in the barn that night when she was. One of them ended up dead and she's the person people want to blame. I don't think she's the criminal here."

Holly put down her cup, leveling a suddenly angry glare at me. "Are you saying my brother had something to do with this?"

"I've never even met your brother. All I know is that the dude skipped town."

"My brother is a good man. He always protected me from guys like Damian and Karl."

"Wait a minute. Why would he have to protect you if you didn't know there was any danger with that crew?"

Before she could answer, the door opened behind me.

Mitch.

He wore gym shorts, a white tee and a Dodgers cap flipped backward. He paused mid-step when he saw us.

"Hey," he said, eyes flicking between us like he was trying to gauge why the hell the air was so dense.

"Hey, babe," Holly greeted. She scurried over to him and slipped a possessive arm around him. "Look who's here. It's Natalie."

I lifted my hand in a half-ass wave with my focus still on my coffee prep. "Hey."

"Small world," she said. "You know, I totally forgot, you used to be a mental patient in one of the wards here. That's how you know Mitch, of course."

Mitch ignored that and addressed me. "What are you doing here?" he asked. "Seeing Tillie?"

"Tillie is so nice," Holly interrupted. "I mean I've met her a few times when Mitch and I socialize. Really a skilled clinician. Just like Mitch here." She smiled up at him and playfully spun his rally cap around. "Oh, but I don't have to tell you that, right?"

"Nope," I said, casually sipping...

"Mitch, you work with Tillie a lot with the tough cases, don't you? Like the addicts and the real lost causes?"

I nearly choked with laughter on my sip of coffee. If sweet little Holly was coming after me, she'd have to try harder. I ate passive aggression for lunch. Mitch of course knew that, which explained his side-eyed glance like he was afraid her attempted sucker pitch was about to be leveled out of the park.

"Yes, unfortunately Mitch has met a few human disasters in his day," I said. "That's pretty much how he met your brother, right?"

And then I just left that right there.

"So, I did have some business here but now I'm done," I declared, popping a cap on my coffee to go. "I'm heading out."

"Thanks for the invite to the auction by the way," Mitch said, his voice stiff, clipped. Professional.

"Sure," I replied. "No problem."

Then Holly opened her mouth.

"We're really happy to be included. I've been saving this cute little pink dress for an event like this. Sounds amazing. And I hope you'll be able to fully enjoy it." She looked at Mitch before continuing, as if sharing a secret. "I know all that rapey stuff must have been horrible. It must be exhausting pretending to be normal all the time."

Mitch's head jerked toward her. Half-shocked, half-disbelieving. "Holly, you can't say stuff like that."

"It's fine, I get what she's saying."

Well played. Ninety percent of me wanted to give her the benefit of the doubt. The other ten saw the glint in her eyes. "I should get going," I said, turning back to the coffee machine. "Traffic's a nightmare."

Mitch took a slow step towards me. "Hey, Nat?"

I looked up.

"Ease up on the coffee. You'll never get to sleep tonight."

His voice cut straight through me. Gentle, low and rough around the edges. Intimate like it used to be.

Holly noticed, too, which was fine because I didn't care what she thought. I gave the weakest smile of my life. "Noted. We'll see you at the auction."

———

Thursday evening. Two days before the big auction and I didn't know what I was wearing. It honestly never crossed my mind, and besides, anything I would want to wear these days wouldn't be black-tie appropriate. Fortunately, when the girls realized I had no wardrobe ideas they called for a fashion emergency, whatever the hell that was, so the beach house became a perfume-soaked situation room. It looked like a tornado had touched down on Rodeo Drive and deposited what it swept up here. Dresses, silk, sequins, satin, flung across the couch, chairs, and even the floor. Tissue paper peeked out of designer garment bags, and hangers clinked as Staci tried to organize the madness by color.

"This one is totally you Nat," Cassidy declared, holding up a slinky scarlet dress that looked like it belonged on a Bond Girl.

I stood on the coffee table while everyone regarded me in a black halter top number so tight around my neck, I thought it would decapitate me. "I guess it's better than this one that screams wardrobe malfunction," I said.

"Cass is right. What about red instead?" Janessa said from the couch, waving a Twizzler in the air for emphasis. "It looks so pretty on you with your blonde hair and your skin tone. Besides it's Valentine's Day. Be festive."

Ari, seated cross-legged on the floor surrounded by brushes and compacts, pointed a mascara wand in my direction. "And we're doing your hair down. Like sexy beach day style."

"No, I have to have my hair up," I said staring into the full-length mirror propped up on the couch to get the "natural light scenario" that according to the rest of them, was important.

"We have to think about makeup too." Ari added. "I'm thinking really smokey eye. Very artistic and dramatic. Lip color TBT."

"You have to look like art! "Cassidy insisted. "Just like on RuPaul's Drag Race."

"The makeup is super important," Ari said. "Now shut up and moisturize."

Staci came into the kitchen with a stack of shoeboxes. "So in my opinion strappy stilettos are the way to go. You have great legs. Let's show off the calves. And as high a heel as you can stand because no offense..."

"I'm really short. I got it." I shrugged. "I do like a good strappy shoe. I'd need to get a pedicure though."

I was in the middle of untying the black satin noose from around my neck when I heard the knock. It was soft, but insistent.

I turned to Cassidy. "Did you order food?"

She shook her head, chewing on a Twizzler. "No, you told me I wasn't allowed anymore after I ordered that whole food truck last week."

I rolled my eyes and went to the door.

Eero.

It looked like he'd just gotten off the team bus. Dress pants and a white button down, although he had removed the required tie and the top button was open at the neck. His usually well-behaved hair fell limp over his eyes. His hand was still raised from knocking. He lowered it slowly as he stepped over the threshold and the room fell silent behind me.

"Hey," he said giving me a curious and subdued once-over. "You look nice. You heading out or something?"

"No, I'm just trying on dresses for Saturday." I reached up and gave him a quick dry kiss he barely returned. "Hi, um I'm happy you're here."

"Where you been, Eero?" Cassidy asked. "Natalie's been back from Buffalo for like three days."

"Cass, filter," Staci hissed, then gave Eero a sympathetic smile. "Hey, how about the rest of us head outside and let you two talk?"

"That's not necessary," I said quickly. "This isn't a thing."

"Actually, Love," Eero interrupted, gently taking my hand, "it is a thing. Do you think we could go somewhere and talk privately? There's stuff I've been thinking about. Stuff I'd like to say."

The strange little quiver in his lower lip told me this was serious, more so than Eero usually allowed himself to be. I nodded. "Sure. Of course."

We headed back to my room. Ari, ever the neat freak, had already reorganized the whole space for me while I was gone. Clean laundry, matched socks, dusted surfaces. I appreciated this because I didn't have to explain yet another one of my short-comings to Eero who I was pretty sure was now convinced I was a few fries short of a Happy Meal.

I sat at the edge of my bed, elbows on my knees, staring at the faint shimmer of ocean through the blinds. He stood near the door for a second, then crossed the room and leaned against the dresser.

"I'm sorry I wasn't around when you got back," he said finally. "I was at a meet. But I kept thinking about you. About everything you must have been dealing with. I just didn't know what to say."

"You don't have to say anything," I assured him.

"But I want to," he said. "That's the thing. I feel like I haven't been the best support. Maybe I don't know how to be. But I want to try."

I looked over at him then, really looked. His face was open, uncertain, like he was attempting a level of serious he never had before.

"I don't expect you to understand," I said gently. "I barely understand it myself. I'm still sorting out what Racer did to me and I'm realizing now I kind of buried all of that for a long time."

Eero nodded slowly. "I get that. Or I'm trying to. And in a lot of ways, that whole physical awful terrible part isn't the biggest issue for me."

"What do you mean?"

He sighed and sat down beside me on the bed. I could tell the way he watched himself rub his palms together he was struggling with finding the right words, so I extra braced myself.

"I need to know what's going on with you and Mitch."

My stomach tightened. I hadn't expected him to go there. At least not so point blank. Hell, I even avoided asking myself the same question because it was too complicated an answer. So, I danced around it with him the same way I did myself. "There's nothing between us. He's just someone I used to know. That's all."

"That may be the way you feel but I don't think that's where he's at." He trailed off and exhaled. "It's like, he knows you. A version of you I'm afraid I never will. Or you won't let me."

"He knows a version of me that doesn't exist anymore," I said.

"I don't want to compete with him, Natalie. If he can help

you in ways I can't, I guess I have to accept that. But I need to know if I'm actually a part of your life or just a placeholder."

"You're not a placeholder," I said, taking his hand and folding it with both of mine. "You're a good person. And I care about you, but I just can't give you everything you want. Not yet. And I know there're girls out there who could give you more, who don't have this baggage, like Paris. She seems to be super into you."

"Paris?" he scoffed. "On the swim team?"

"And if she's what you want, I won't hold it against you."

He slipped off the bed and crouched in front of me staring at our fingers entwined in my lap. "Look, I don't really care about Paris or any other girl who's out there. What I want is you. And we can take it slow. It doesn't have to be serious or scary. I just want to know there's room for me in your life."

"There is," I whispered. "If you're willing to be patient."

He kissed my knuckles, soft and sure. "I can be patient."

I watched the relief wash over his face. Whatever he was looking for, reassurance, validation, I was happy I hit all those notes for him. After a moment he reached into the pocket of his pants and pulled out a small box.

Jewelry.

Shit.

He opened my fisted right hand and placed it in my palm. "I found this at a little shop by the beach. It's no big deal. It just made me think of you."

I snapped the box open. Inside was a necklace, a silver charm in the shape of an ocean wave. "This is beautiful, "I said, slipping my fingers through it and holding it up in the light.

"I thought you might want to carry the water with you. Even when you're away from it."

I stared at it, then at him. "You're kind of the best."

He grinned. "Thanks."

I shook my head, laughing under my breath. He sat behind me and put it on. His fingers grazed my neck. I didn't flinch. "Will you come to the auction with me?" I asked. "It means a lot to me and not just because it's Annie's foundation. But because I want to try. One good night is a start."

He reached for my hand, pausing an inch before touching. I gave a small nod. His fingers laced with mine, gently. "Then that's what we'll do," he said. "One good night."

I squeezed his hand. My voice came out soft, but sure, "Okay."

We stayed like that, sitting on the edge of the bed as the night deepened around us. Not needing anything more than quiet and honesty. Eero's hand was warm in mine. Solid. Grounding. He showed up, and maybe that's all I needed.

SEVENTEEN

BY THE TIME Saturday rolled around, the beach house was in full chaos mode. It was too small a space to contain Cassidy's aggressive bathroom takeovers, Staci and Ari's ongoing heel-vs-flat debate, and Janessa's perfume-exploding-in-her-swim-duffle drama so they decided we needed more space to prep. The mayhem didn't bother me. In fact, it was oddly comforting. Like pre-meet jitters before a big race. This was a big deal, after all.

Staci arranged for the private suite on the top floor of the gallery. Once in a while, people rented out the space for wedding receptions, and the upstairs was reserved for the wedding party's dressing room of sorts. This worked out perfectly for me. I had a place to time out and recharge if all the "people-ing" required a break.

So, I stood in front of the floor to ceiling mirror regarding myself in my bright red dress, deciding if I was bold enough to wear my hair down. Janessa had curled it just in case. All I needed to do was pluck out a few bobby pins. Smokey eyes, with strip lashes, a red lip. I even had my nails done in a classy French mani with little white rhinestones. If I was the ringleader of this pony show, I would have to be seen. I wanted to step into this. Wear this dress. Let my hair down.

Show up for Annie. Show up for myself.

I was teasing a newly freed curl when Staci slipped into the room. She was already dressed in a shimmering silver floor-length gown that hugged her in all the right places. Her red hair was swept up in a loose bun with tendrils framing her face. She looked fierce and stunning, the embodiment of Valentine's Day glam.

"Okay, just talked to Rain downstairs." She waved her phone in the air. "Everything's on track. Caterers are setting up, musicians are tuning, bartenders are getting their stations sorted. Everyone else is downstairs waiting for people to arrive."

I heaved a breath. "Wow. So, this is it, huh?"

She looked at me in the mirror and smiled. "You look good, Nat. I'm so happy you settled on this dress. Strapless and the poofy skirt that shows off your legs. And your hair down..." She gave a dramatic chef's kiss and wink. "Perfect Valentine's Day vibe. You look like a princess."

"Thanks."

Staci stepped closer, her eyes catching the glint of the necklace resting just above the neckline of my gown. "Wait, what's this?"

I reached up, touching the tiny silver charm. "It's pretty, right? Eero gave it to me. He found it at one of those jewelry shops by the beach. He said it was so I could carry the water with me, even when I'm away from it."

Staci's face softened. "That's actually really sweet."

"I thought so, too," I said quietly. "Listen, I just wanted to apologize to you for keeping a lot of stuff to myself. I think I might be really ready to start over. This..." I gestured to the dress, the necklace, the night ahead, "...is me trying."

She didn't speak right away, and when I met her eyes in the mirror she looked like she might cry. "You don't have to pretend you're fine with me. Not tonight. Not ever," she said. "And if you are struggling, I want to know. You don't have to hide from me."

"I won't. And the same goes for you, bestie."

We walked arm in arm to the stairs but paused at the top when we saw what awaited us at the bottom. We were awestruck. The gallery shimmered with candlelight, red rose flower arrangements. Ice sculptures, champagne fountains. Waiters glided past with trays of champagne and fancy food. Music floated up from a quartet tucked near the far wall, something classical but not stuffy. Spotlights danced across walls of abstract pieces and moody sculptures, everything sleek and curated.

"Holy extravagant," I mumbled to her. "How the fuck did this all happen?"

Staci shrugged. "That's how charity works. It makes people feel good to help." She pointed over toward one of the dessert tables. Tillie, in a beautiful black cocktail dress, was chatting it up with an older woman in a long grey gown.

"Holy crap, is that Cassidy's Aunt Rose?" I asked.

"Sure is." Staci laughed. "She and Tillie hit it off when they met discussing Cassidy's living situation. She also is a big fan of modern art, so that helps, too."

"Wow, so many people."

"You're still a big deal, Natalie. An international athlete with a compelling story." She paused with a sigh. "And not to throw you shade but it kind of doesn't hurt that some of the pieces tonight are from Damian Cross' collection."

I think she thought that would offend me somehow. That the fanfare over the murder case would trump my celebrity influence. I was confident that Annie would agree with me that money was green wherever it came from. And this was going to a good cause. "Where is Marradine anyway?" I asked. "I probably should have picked her up myself."

"Rain is arranging that," Staci assured me. "No worries. Come on."

We descended below as people arrived from the front entrance. Black ties, fancy gowns. A few celebrities. Many friends. Toward the back I could see security guards chatting with limo drivers, and press photogs fumbling with their cameras. Eero waited for me at the bottom step. He held out his hand to me and kissed my cheek.

"Wow," Eero said, walking a slow circle around me. "You're a knockout, Love."

"Thank you," I said, giving him an appreciative once-over. He was in a tailored black suit, no tie, and his dark hair slicked back dashing European cologne ad style. "You clean up okay yourself."

Ari, Cassidy, and Janessa made their way over to us, each with drink in hand and in Cassidy's case, food in the other. Ari and Janessa both opted for short, similar shaded pink dresses for Valentine's Day, while Cassidy went with red like mine. Even her cute little number had to have a discrete pocket at her hip to carry around her trusty "control life" remote.

"Staci says I have to go help Lance mingle and shmooze," I informed everyone.

"That's absolutely correct," Staci declared, giving the room a quick scan. "You can make small talk for an hour and then just enjoy the party."

"I heard there were celebrities showing up," Janessa said. "I mean other than you, of course."

Suddenly, I was super-focused on one guest in particular. He stood near the sculpture alcove, nursing a whiskey and talking to Lance. Even from across the room, I felt his dark slippery-like-an-eel vibe. Lance caught my eye and motioned me over. Staci and Eero followed.

"Natalie," Karl said with a warm, crooked grin. He worked the charm, head cocked, chest puffed out. He dropped his empty glass on a passing waiter's tray and pulled out a pack of cigarettes from his breast pocket. "I was just telling Lance what a stunning turnout this is. You've done an incredible job."

"We appreciate the contributions to the auction," Staci said coolly. "The paintings from Damian's estate have drawn a lot of interest."

Karl waved a dismissive hand. "Just glad to help a good cause. Damian would've wanted that."

"You can't smoke those in here sir," A waiter passing by said to him politely. "Sorry."

"Oh, yes of course." He jammed the cigarettes back in his pocket and pulled out a tin of mints instead. "You've got a hell of a crowd tonight," he said popping one in his mouth. "Hope the bidding gets wild."

Then he was gone, slipping off into the sea of well-dressed bodies.

"He's creepy as fuck," Ari grumbled.

"Hey, so when does the band start?" Eero asked, changing the subject. "That's the plan, right? Do a good deed and then party till midnight?"

"The auction is in about an hour," Lance informed us. "Eating, drinking, dancing and romancing can be done any time before that."

"How about I grab us some desserts," Eero asked. "They have those little fruit cakes that remind me of back home. You want one? Get your strength up for the dance floor."

Before I could answer, I caught sight of the beautiful couple in the center of a large group's attention. Holly and Mitch stood near the main gallery space, standing just off to the right of a large installation with a few of the Dunes' staff. She wore a pale blush dress that sparkled like sugar crystals. Her hair was swept back, makeup soft and polished. Every inch the elegant girlfriend. And Mitch...

Damn.

Tailored tux. No tie. That perfect GQ-level five o'clock shadow. He stood like he owned the room, shoulders loose, posture confident, a slow smirk curling at the edge of his mouth. I could tell he was deep into one of his dramatic stories the way he gestured with his hands. His audience looked downright enchanted. I understood. I'd been there.

And then...

It appeared he stopped talking mid-sentence. Time froze. My heart stopped. His eyes trained on me in hyper-focus.

He didn't smile. He didn't wave. Just a small, deliberate nod and a flick of two fingers wrapped around his champagne glass. A signal only I would recognize.

Eero gave me a little tug of my hand. "We should probably go over there. Don't you think?"

"No," I said too quickly. "It's fine."

"Natalie!" Holly waved her hand in the air flashing the sweetest smile.

The thing about this girl was that I couldn't tell if this was her being nice or diabolically manipulative. I wondered if that thought reflected worse on me than it did her. Before Eero or I could avoid the scene, the four of us were among the small group. He tensed beside me, not that I could blame him. This was the moment we'd both been trying to avoid.

"Thank you so much again for coming tonight," I said to the horseshoe of smiling faces. I decided to dust off my classic (fallen) American Sweetheart persona for tonight's gig. Extra perk and pep for good measure. I shook hands and conversated politely, but I could tell I was rusty. It made me grateful for the loudish music in the background because it drowned out the quiver in my voice.

"Natalie," Holly said brightly. "You look amazing. The red dress is so brave."

Brave. Right. "Thanks," I said, managing a smile. "You look great, too."

Holly beamed, brushing her hair back. "Valentine's glamour, right? A good effort." She looked at Eero, adding, "And you're her boyfriend, I assume?"

He nodded politely and offered a hand. "Eero, Nice to meet you."

"Oh, you have an accent," Holly said as if finding anything to say to avoid silence. "Where are you from and what brings you here?"

"Spain," he replied. "I swim. And I'm fortunate enough to train with both the fastest and the most beautiful athlete in the world."

Eero made a dramatic show of brushing my hair off my shoulder, his fingers lingering just long enough to draw a round of playful "awws" from the onlookers. Everyone seemed charmed except Mitch, who with narrowed eyes tracked the motion of Eero's hand as it slid around my waist.

"You two seem very happy together," Holly chimed in, her voice syrupy and sharp at the edges. "And tonight's such a win. Everything came together so perfectly. We're thrilled to be here, right Mitch?"

He blinked, like he'd just showed back up from somewhere else entirely. "What?"

"The auction," she said with a tight smile. "It's a success, right?"

Mitch gave a small, distracted nod. "Yes. Absolutely." His

attention snapped back to me. "I'm sorry, but Natalie, can I steal you for a moment? Just for one dance?"

My stomach flipped. I nervously turned toward Eero, and he surprised me with a wink. "Go ahead," he said softly. "It's just a dance."

"Then, shall we?" Mitch offered his arm, and he guided us to the center of the floor. The crowd parted as we moved through it. All eyes were on us, but with him at my side, I didn't mind. I felt confident. Secure. The music slipped into something slow and sultry thick with feeling. The lights dimmed, the mood shifted.

The moment he pulled me in close I forgot how to breathe. He laced his fingers with mine and pressed our joined hands gently to his chest. I could feel the rise and fall of him, the quiet thump of his heartbeat. I rested my cheek against it, just so I could listen.

"You look incredible," he said, his breath ruffling the top of my hair.

"Good lighting," I half-assed joked. "And so do you. Very... stoic FBI chic."

We moved slowly, effortlessly, our bodies falling into sync like they remembered each other. We'd danced like this before at that wedding in Long Beach and a university gala when he got his PhD. I remembered the weight of his hand on my back, how his touch always landed with precision, never forced. Just enough. Safe. Intimate. Familiar.

For a few seconds, the rest of the room blurred. There was no Eero. No Holly. No crowd. Just us.

"I was hoping I could get you alone, tonight," he said. "I wanted to talk to you."

There was a weird intensity to his voice. I tilted my head up to look at him. "Are you okay?"

He nodded. I didn't buy it.

"Are you sure?"

"Look, I miss you, Natalie," he blurted. "And I've tried to let everything go between us because I thought that's what you wanted or needed, but I don't want to pretend anymore." His grip tightened around me. "You told me you're putting a pause on some things, like school and swimming, and I want you to know I support that. Whatever you need..."

"Mitch, please tell me what you're getting at?"

He looked down at me to meet my gaze. "Natalie, I..."

And then, suddenly, his forehead wrinkled, in confusion, disappointment, anger, I wasn't sure. Like a dark cloud settled over him. Finally, he released me and stepped back just enough to stare at the charm at my throat. The silver wave necklace. Eero's gift.

"That's new," he said, voice low.

I reached up, self-consciously brushing it with my fingers. "Yeah. It was a Valentine's gift. From Eero."

He didn't respond. His eyes lingered there a second longer then drifted back to mine. All that softness in him twisted into something else. A quiet break under the surface. "Wow...okay," he stammered.

It was like he was having a conversation with himself. A deep one I didn't want to interrupt. Finally, he exhaled like whatever he was grappling with was resolved. "Answer me honestly, does he give you what you need, Nat? Really?"

The knot in my throat tightened. "I don't know. I guess he tries."

"Yeah...right." His voice faded, the sentence unfinished, like he didn't trust himself to go further.

"Mitch, please," I pleaded, my hand fisting around his shirt. "Please just tell me what it is you want?"

I felt a finger tap lightly on my shoulder. When I turned, heart pounding in my ears, I expected to see Eero, or maybe even Holly ready with a leash, but it was Lance. His face was tight with panic, the lines around his eyes deeper than usual.

"I'm sorry to interrupt you two but Nat, I need you. Now."

Mitch straightened, instantly alert. "Everything okay?"

"I'm not sure, but it's important," Lance said quickly, then focused on me again. "Marradine is here, and she has something for you. She wants to give it to you immediately."

EIGHTEEN

LANCE WAS ALREADY MOVING toward the side hallway near the private offices. I followed, the heavy rustle of my dress trailing behind me.

"She got here about ten minutes ago," Lance said over his shoulder. "Snuck in through the staff entrance. Said she needed to see you before anything else."

The closer we got to the office, the quieter everything became. The party noise faded into a dull murmur, like it was happening in another world entirely.

When he pushed open the office door, I stopped cold.

Marradine was sitting in one of the chairs, her legs tucked up underneath her, notebook in her lap. Her hair was loose and wavy around her face, and she wore the simple black cocktail dress Staci and I sent to her. Not rehab khakis. Not anything from the Dunes at all.

When she saw me, there was no acknowledgement, but her eyes were wide and watchful. Like she wasn't sure if she should bolt or shout or cry. Her fingers tightened around the edges of her notebook, but she didn't speak. She didn't need to.

"Hey," I said as I sat down in the chair across from her. She didn't look away. "I'm happy you showed up. The dress looks good."

She ignored the small talk, instead opening her notebook to a center page. Inside there were two Dunes envelopes. She placed them both on the table side by side and slid me the one on the right first.

This felt important. Something life-changing maybe. With slightly shaking hands, I opened the envelope. The paper inside was smooth, standard white but somehow that felt dramatic, like everything Marradine ever put into the world. The handwriting was hers. Uneven, a little rushed. But clear.

You're facing your demons. Now I'll face mine. I didn't mean for any of this.

But I remember it now.

And then came the next envelope. This one felt heavier. Like the stock of paper inside was thicker than usual. I broke open the seal, unfolded it, stared at it.

Then looked at Marradine.

"You drew this?" I asked, voice low and reverent.

She nodded once. Just barely.

And then it registered. I answered my own question. "You *lived* this," I whispered. "You were there."

I looked at her again, really looked. She didn't seem like a patient anymore. Not like the fragile girl scribbling in the margins. She seemed like someone who had clawed her way back from the edge and found the strength to bring the truth with her. "You okay with people seeing this?" I asked her quietly. Because you know what's gonna happen when they do. There's no going back."

She reached for her notebook, scribbled something quickly, and turned it toward me.

Not okay. But I have to.

I stood, envelope in hand, and looked around the room. "Let's do this."

When I stepped out into the hall, Staci and Eero stood there, looking panic-stricken like I was about to deliver some grave diagnosis. Oddly enough, I didn't feel that way. Not for Marradine. I felt...calm.

"Well?" Staci asked. "What's the deal? What did she tell you?"

Behind her, the auction was in full swing. Shoulder-to-shoulder crowds clustered around the artwork. Lance was mid-speech, giving some curated pitch of the final pieces. A room of unsuspecting spectators with no idea what was coming.

"Call 911 and say there's been a car accident outside," I said casually to Eero. "We have enough security for now, but we'll need backup soon."

"Backup for what?" Eero asked.

"Make sure the Untethered collection goes last," I told Staci. "And have Rain find a projector."

Staci disappeared with a nod, while I stood guard at the office door. Eero gave me a once-over, clearly fighting the urge to ask a thousand questions.

"What do you want me to do?" he asked, more gently this time.

"Just be with me," I said. "That's all."

The lights inside the gallery dimmed slowly, like the beginning of a curtain call. Lance had billed the Untethered series as the night's grand finale. Totally exploitative, but it would raise the most money for the foundation. And now, it felt like the perfect Hollywood climax. The chatter faded to murmurs, champagne flutes stilled, and all eyes shifted to the small platform in the gallery's center.

Eero's hand brushed against mine. I didn't take it, yet. My fingers still clutched the envelope Marradine had given me. I passed the sketch to Rain with instructions to prep the projector. There was no turning back now.

You're facing your demons. Now I'll face mine.

Lance took the mic, his hand tight on the edge of the podium. He looked calm, but I knew him well enough to see the tension hiding beneath.

"Ladies and gentlemen," he began, voice smooth but firm, "before we close out this incredible evening, we have one final piece to share. It's not listed in the program. It was delivered tonight by the artist herself."

Staci leaned in behind me. "The artist? Who the hell is the artist?"

I allowed myself a small smile. "You'll see."

Lance glanced down at the sketch in his hand, fingers trembling. "It's a pencil drawing. A moment captured from memory, vivid, painful, and brave. It's deep. Personal. And we are lucky enough to have a greater insight tonight. The artist asked that we let her speak about her own creative impressions and what exactly inspired them."

A hush settled over the room as Marradine stepped into the spotlight. She wore the simple black dress, hair pulled back, no makeup. Raw. Honest. Real. I felt Eero shift beside me and glanced over. I didn't know if he knew anything about art auctions, but he damn sure could sense something crazy was about to go down.

"Hello everyone, remember me? I'm Marradine Addison. Most of you looked shocked to see me. Or maybe you're just shocked to see me here because the last you heard, the news was reporting I lost my mind. That I was in rehab, or in jail, or dead." Marradine cleared her throat and shifted. "I'm not just a name in the tabloids or a post in your feed. I'm a person. I exist. I feel. I create."

A few murmurs rippled through the audience. A couple of

journalists crept closer, red lights on their phones blinking to life.

"Most of you came tonight for the Untethered collection, I'm sure. That's the whole point, right? Be lured by the mystery around Damian Cross' murder? Well let me tell you..." her tears started out of nowhere, but she sniffled and soldered on. "Damian was a good man, and while these four pieces were credited to the Damian Cross collection, the artist is not anonymous. I painted them. And I'm ready to own that now."

"What is she doing?" Staci whispered.

"I don't know," I said, eyes fixed on Marradine. "But I think we need to let her finish."

Marradine nodded toward the velvet curtain hiding the projection screen. "There's one more piece tonight. The last of the Untethered series. You see the collection itself features a girl scared, confused, out of place. I'm sure you caught on to the narrative. Anyway, she's someone I relate to." She paused and heaved a deep breath. "This last of this collection is not a painting but rather a simple pencil sketch. It's the final part of her story."

And then, the curtain dropped. The projector flickered to life.

The image that filled the screen sucked the air from the room.

"This is a painting depicting the Damian Cross murder." Her voice cracked but she kept going. "I was there that night in the barn when it happened. And this is what I saw."

It was stark. Harsh. Deep heavy black on white paper. The strokes were rough, jagged with angry emotion, but the image was stark clear. A barn. Two men. One slumped forward, knees buckling. The other behind him, pulling a rope of some sort around his neck. In the foreground was a spilled jar of paintbrushes, a half-finished canvas. Background demons in dark shadows.

Gasps erupted around us.

"Karl Rollings drugged me and assaulted me," Marradine said, her voice cracking. "It wasn't the first time. But that night, I was in the barn, painting. Karl thought I was alone. Damian caught him. They fought. Karl strangled him with a leather horse lead from the back stall."

The gallery fell into stunned silence. Even Eero went pale beside me. "This is crazy," he whispered.

I followed his gaze. Karl Rollings stood across the room, frozen beneath the gallery lights. His glass of whiskey dangled loosely in his hand. His face had gone ghostly pale, jaw slack. He didn't move. Just stared.

Marradine went on, steadier now. "He killed Damian. I didn't remember it for a long time. But I do now."

Security moved fast. Two guards appeared seemingly out of nowhere and approached Karl from opposite sides. One took the glass from his hand, the other touched his arm gently butfirmly. Karl didn't resist. He didn't say a word. His eyes never left the projection.

Marradine stepped back, trembling but defiant. Phones were out. People whispered. My friends crowded around me, Staci, Ari, Cassidy, Janessa. All wide-eyed, speechless.

"Holy shit," Cassidy muttered. "We just solved the freaking Damian Cross murder."

I looked at Marradine, who looked right back. Her hands were shaking, but her chin was high. She had spoken her truth, not with words, but with the only language she fully trusted. Art. It was the most honest performance she ever delivered.

———

The beach house was quiet, except for the occasional pop of ocean wind against the windows and the low hum of the air conditioner. Everyone had kicked off their shoes hours ago, and we were all scattered across the living room in varying stages of exhaustion. The mood felt very much like friends in a lifeboat awaiting rescue. Speechless, stunned. Too tired to sleep and eager to hear the update of how the hell it all ended once Lance came back from the gallery.

"I can't believe all that fucking happened," Ari finally said half-collapsed on the kitchen table. "You seriously had no idea Marradine was gonna pull something like that?" she asked Staci beside her.

"How would I?" Staci insisted with her head in her hands. "Besides Natalie is the one who arranged all this. She had the inside information."

"I didn't arrange anything," I insisted. I sat cross-legged near the fireplace next to a half- asleep Eero. I was nursing a ginger ale and still in my red gown balancing his head on my shoulder. "I knew something was up with her, but I didn't know it was all that."

Cassidy peeked her head out from under the blanket on the floor. "Dramatic murder case confessions like that happen all the time. Classic Dateline."

Janessa stood by the sliding glass door just shaking her head incredulously. "You guys sure know how to throw a party."

Finally, Lance came through the door, still in his suit, loosened tie, hair askew. We all turned to him like we awaited the town crier's declaration. We wanted to know our fate.

"Well?" Staci prompted.

Lance grabbed a bottled water from the fridge and took a long swig. He cleared his throat. "So," he said. "Police are gone, and the gallery is all cleaned up. And as far as the auction went, while I don't have exact numbers, preliminary estimates say Annie's foundation did well. Like...really well."

Everyone perked up. Ari clapped. Cassidy grinned.

"How well is well?" Janessa mumbled, barely lifting her head.

"We'll know for sure tomorrow," Lance said. "But I think it's safe to say we crushed it."

"Annie would've loved it," I said, feeling super prideful. "It felt like a real celebration of her."

"And let's be honest," Janessa said, sitting down at the table with Staci and Ari, "the murder reveal didn't exactly hurt the press coverage."

Ari chuckled. "Yeah, nothing says fundraising success like the live arrest of a cold-blooded killer."

"Still," Lance added, his voice gentler, "I feel for Marradine. That was brave. I know it wasn't easy."

"She's staying at the Dunes for now," I said, more to myself than anyone. "Tillie's going to keep working with her. And the staff will keep the media away. At least as much as they can."

"She's got people in her corner now," Staci added. "For the first time, maybe ever."

"Speaking of people in their corner," Cassidy piped up, voice perky despite the late hour, "Aunt Rose had the time of her life tonight. She loves a good snooty party."

We all laughed at that.

"She flirted with two of the caterers and tried to buy one of the musicians," Cassidy added proudly.

"She did not," Staci groaned, but she was smiling. "She did buy a couple pieces though. That was cool of her."

A beat passed, then Ari sat up suddenly engaged by her new thought. "So you guys really think Holly didn't know more? I mean, she was there that night. She knew Karl and Damian."

"She did seem genuinely rattled," Eero added. "Even I could tell that."

"Holly's not evil," I said. "Just naïve. And I think she wants to be helpful, but she's scared of saying the wrong thing."

"Well," Lance said, pushing away from the counter, "Brody Inez is flying back from Europe next week to be deposed. That should be something."

Ari perked up. "You think he knows what really went on between Karl and Damian?"

"He was in business with both of them," Lance said. "He knows something. Whether he'll say it under oath is another story."

"I'd love to see that slimeball crack," Janessa muttered.

I rubbed the charm at my neck absentmindedly. It was still there, Eero's little silver wave. Somehow, that tiny thing was grounding me.

"So," Staci said, eyes moving around the room. "What's next for all of us?"

We all went quiet. Not heavy quiet. Just that tired, lingering kind. The kind you feel when something big ends, and the next thing is waiting but hasn't quite started. Staci went to Lance and put her arms around him. "I guess we'll keep building the gallery. And we'll help with the foundation, of course."

"Thanks," I said. "Sounds like a plan."

"I'll keep working on my own stuff." Lance took a gulp of his water. "Keep trying to get my name out there."

"I'll keep flying," Ari said.

Cassidy yawned. "And I think I'm gonna rewatch some of the old Jeopardy episodes. I'm starting to really like vintage gameshows."

"I think I'm going to train for the next Olympics," I blurted.

When I scanned the silent room, every eye was on me. I

couldn't decide if it was shock or disbelief or maybe waiting for the punchline.

Eero smiled at me. "I wondered when you would come back to that. Are you serious, Love?"

"Yeah. I'm serious. I figured I'm out of school for a while anyway and to do this requires all my time. I miss swimming and I feel good when I'm in the pool. I think it's what makes sense." I felt the weight of the words settle. "No more false starts."

"That's badass," Cassidy said.

Staci nodded. "I love that for you."

"I do, too," Eero hugged me tight, and I leaned into it.

Ari raised her bottle. "To new chapters."

We all raised our drinks in the lazy, quiet way people do when they've survived something. One by one people peeled out or headed to bed. Janessa went home. Eero helped me clean up the kitchen before finally saying goodbye at the door.

"Quite a night, huh?" he said. "You Americans love your drama. It's so good to know you'll be back in the pool where you belong. We could train together."

I took his hands and gave them a squeeze. "Yeah, then you wouldn't need Paris around anymore to keep you company."

"You don't have to worry about Paris," he said. "You don't have to worry about anyone. You own the pool, and you know it. I'm a lucky guy to share your lane if you let me."

He kissed me and I could tell by the slight tremble, he was holding himself back which I appreciated. He gave me a wink before he walked out the door. "See you tomorrow, Love."

The house was finally quiet.

Everyone else had drifted off to bed, but I was still awake— wired, restless, spinning in a fog of adrenaline and clarity. The cameras, the chaos. Annie's foundation. Cassidy. Eero. So many lives shifted tonight.

And I wanted mine to shift, too. Not by accident, not by trauma, but by choice.

I was in the kitchen ready to snap off the lights when the sliding glass door opened behind me.

Mitch.

"Hey," he whispered. "I wasn't sure if you'd be up."

"I haven't really been down," I said, tossing a dish towel onto the counter. "Come on in."

He wore sneakers, jeans, and a navy sweatshirt with the sleeves pushed up to his elbows. His hair was damp, like he'd just showered and he was cleanshaven. I felt kind of sloppy, still in my dress. God only knew what my hair and makeup looked like.

He stepped in and leaned against the counter; arms folded against himself. "I'm sorry to come by so late. It's been a crazy night."

"Sure has."

"I just needed to talk to you." He stared at his feet. "We were sort of interrupted when we were dancing."

There was a tremor to his voice, an anxiety there. Like something weighed on his mind. "What?" I asked. "Is something wrong? Is Holly okay? I'm sure what happened tonight rattled her cage a little."

"She's all right. She's with her parents." After a moment he held out his hand to me. "Come take a walk on the beach with me. Just for a few minutes. Please?"

"Of course." I slipped my feet into a pair of flip flops, and we walked hand in hand down the back steps, out onto the beach. The sand was cool and soft, the moon washing the scene with silver. "I'm glad you're here," I said, hoping to lighten his oddly mellow mood. "I want to tell you something that I'm kind of excited about."

He turned to me, brows raised slightly.

"I've decided to start training again," I said. "For real. Not just conditioning or pool time. I'm going back to Matthews this week."

His eyes widened. "Training? Like—"

"Back to the Olympics," I said. "I'm going all in."

He stopped walking. The moon hit his face just enough to catch the shift in his expression. "You're serious?"

I nodded. "I want it. Still. After everything. I still want this."

"That's...damn. Natalie, that's incredible." He pulled me in a tight embrace and I let myself fall into it. "I'm proud of you," he said, rocking me slowly with his chin resting on the top of my head. "God, I am so proud of you."

We stood there in silence, the waves crashing softly in the background, the moon's glow hitting us like a spotlight. Then he exhaled one of those low, resigned breaths that said, *I hate to be the one to tell you this but..."*

"I've got news, too," he said.

I looked up at him. His eyes fixed past me at the ocean. "What?" I asked.

"I'm leaving. Got orders this morning."

The words registered but barely. I slid my hands across his broad chest, my fingers finding the ties of his hoodie to fidget with. "Leaving where? And what do you mean orders?"

"San Diego for now, then maybe overseas. Not a deployment, not yet anyway, but it's months. Maybe more."

"Oh." I shook my head attempting to recover from the bomb he just dropped. "Wait, I didn't think this would ever happen. You're a shrink not a soldier."

"I'm both now, Natalie. That's part of this new job."

"Right. Of course." I stepped away from him and hugged myself against a sudden chill.

"It's not...it's not what I wanted tonight to be," he admitted. "I thought it was Valentine's Day and maybe a new start..."

"A new start for who?" I met his eyes. "Wait a minute, tonight, when we were dancing. You were going to tell me this. Were you going to ask me to go with you?"

We stared at each other for a long time. There we were, two people with too much history and not enough resolution. I stepped forward first, laying my hand back over the familiar beat of his heart. He wrapped his arms around me and again pulled me close. "You looked beautiful tonight," he said. His voice was thick, a little unsteady. "I always loved your hair down."

I smiled against him. He knew what wearing my hair loose meant for me.

"And what you did for Marradine," he kissed the top of my head. "You know how many people look up to you? You inspire?"

I playfully pushed him away and laughed. "Stop, you're crazy."

"Crazy about some things I guess." He sighed like that was an admission of sorts then gently reached for the silver charm at my neck, the wave Eero had given me.

"Make sure he treats you right," he said, voice barely audible. "You deserve that."

I looked up at him, studying the shadowed lines of his face. "I will."

And then, without another word, he kissed me.

It wasn't passionate or desperate. It was deep and slow, aching with bad timing and missed opportunity. His fingers tangled in my hair, brushing it back from my cheek with a reverence that destroyed me.

When we parted, his lips hovered near mine, breath trembling. "That wasn't a goodbye kiss," he whispered.

"I know," I said.

He stepped back and walked off into the night, footsteps fading into sand and surf until he disappeared.

I didn't stop him.

EPILOGUE

THE POOL LOOKED SMALLER than I remembered. Or maybe I'd just grown a little since the last time I was here.

The smell of bromine hit me like a bittersweet nostalgia. It burned the back of my throat and stung my nose in the best possible way. Above me, the early morning sun filtered through the skylights, painting gold on the water's surface. Calm. Chill.

I stood at the edge, towel over one shoulder, suit tight, cap on. My nerves hummed under my skin, but they didn't feel like fear. They felt like fuel. Like I was exactly where I was supposed to be.

This was my house.

Coach Matthews stood near the far end, barking times at a trio of younger swimmers doing drills. He still wore the same navy tracksuit and the same battered stopwatch around his neck, like no time had passed at all. But it had. A lot of it to me but in reality, only weeks.

"You ready to take this seriously again?" he asked, squinting at me across the blocks. "You mean it this time?"

I nodded. "More than ever."

He looked me over. Not judgmental, never that, but

focused. Curious, maybe, about what was so different now. What was driving me. There was a laundry list of things, no time to mention. I felt for my silver water wave charm at my neck. Enough talk. It was go time.

"You look stronger," he said after a beat.

"I am."

He clicked the stopwatch in his hand and pointed toward the blocks. "Let's see what you've got."

I walked toward the starting platform; my feet bare against the cold tile. I passed a row of swimmers stretching and chatting and for once, I didn't feel like I had something to prove. Or something to hide. The past three years had felt like a wreck in slow motion. Leaving the Dunes, getting swallowed whole by college, trying to outrun a past I couldn't shake. There were times I thought I was broken beyond repair. But the truth was, every crash, every panic attack, every time I'd let myself unravel in front of the people who stayed, it all brought me here. To this block. This moment.

None of it was wasted. Not a second.

I climbed onto the platform. My toes curled over the rubber edge. The world narrowed to my lane, black line and blue. Clear and steady in the still water.

This was the new beginning.

I bent down low. Took my mark.

And when the whistle blew, I let myself fly.

ACKNOWLEDGMENTS

Thank you Kari and Barb for being the most awesome besties a girl could have! You are the best beta readers and the most talented writers I know! Jill Stadler, editor extraordinaire you are a magician, and your knowledge of Southern California is incredible!! What would I do without you?

Notes From The Deep End

Treading Water

False Start

ABOUT THE AUTHOR

Daniella Blue has been a writer her whole life, penning her first story in purple crayon at the age of seven. When not at her computer, Daniella can be found on the golf course, tennis court, ski slope and occasionally the bowling alley. She is considering training for a triathlon. Other favorite activities include obsessing over classic 80's TV and getting her nails done. She lives in western New York with her three boys and two Dachshunds. Purple is still her favorite color.